Connie,
   Happy reading!

SHADOW IN THE WOODS

J.P. Choquette

Other books by J.P. Choquette

Epidemic
Dark Circle
Subversion
Restitution

Cover Design: The Cover Collection
Formatting: Polgarus Studio

ISBN-13: 978-1977680471
ISBN-10: 197768047X

Dedication

To Beth Kanell, a true kindred spirit and without whom this book would never have seen the light of day.

Acknowledgements

Many thanks to my wonderful readers, especially to Erin Chagnon, Pam Irish, Ann Kalinoski, and Angela Lavery, each of whom worked hard to make this a better book. I value your insights during an early read through. Thank you for taking time from your busy schedules to help with this book.

Thanks too, to Helen Baggott, my editor extraordinaire who caught lots of "little things" that would have added up to big things. It was a pleasure working with you.

To all the readers who continue to inquire about the "next book," and hold my toes to the fire—in a good way—thank you.

And of course, my deep appreciation and love to my family. Serge, you are my perfect match and I'm so grateful you're in my life. Pascal, you are a gift from above. Thank you both for your patience and support as I frantically write what the voices in my head tell me to. I'm honored to be called your wife and mother, respectively.

~Dios Amore~

November 1, 1889—*The Green Mountain Daily*

Mrs. Veronica Brown of Little River, seeks information on the disappearance of her daughter, Miss Lilian Brown. Widow of the late Charles Brown, an esteemed banker in the Little River area, Mrs. Brown is distraught over her fourteen-year-old daughter's disappearance.

Miss Brown was last seen walking on the logging road east of Little River, and was wearing a red hat and brown coat.

Hunters in the area stated that they had seen an animal of some kind, perhaps a bear, but no evidence has been found to signify that Miss Brown met an untimely death. The local sheriff's department, along with townsfolk, have been searching the area, but no signs of the missing girl have yet been found.

April 17, 1971—*The Green Mountain Daily*

"It were big, I can tell you that." These words were recorded during an interview of Reginald Jarvis, a local resident of Little River. On the evening of April 16th, Jarvis states that he was walking along the logging road just outside of Little River when he saw what he calls a "Sasquatch."

"I never seen nothing like it in all my days on God's green earth," Mr. Jarvis stated. "It stood up on two legs just like you and me, but was covered in fur. Looked like of them big apes at the zoo."

Residents in the area have been warned by authorities to take additional care with their trash cans and to cease feeding birds at backyard birdfeeders. They suspect that a bear has come out of hibernation early.

To that Jarvis says, "Ain't never seen no bear looked like that."

Chapter One

Maria Rodriguez woke feeling as though she'd been running all night long. Her hair was tangled; a sweaty film lay across the back of her neck and knees. In her dreams, she had been running, chased once again by someone, or something, bad. When she was young her mother told her she had a sixth sense. Every morning Maria woke with this heavy twist of fear in her gut, and hoped her mother was wrong. That bad things really weren't lurking around corners waiting for her.

She rolled over, the air chilly after the sweltering blankets. Maria pushed her hair away from her face and sat on the edge of the bed, her finger pulling back the window shade. Outside, small puddles of sunlight formed on the already drying grass and piles of leaves. Vermont was beautiful in the fall and this was a day that was postcard-perfect.

For other girls, childhood had been filled with brightly colored balloons, lazy afternoons in the sun, dreaming about fairy tale endings. They had played dress up in gowns as frothy as cupcake icing, picturing themselves in Hollywood or on Broadway. Not Maria. For her, childhood was an endless maze of dark tunnels, all of the *what ifs* and *it could happens* a constant weight on her shoulders.

"Break a mirror and it's seven years of bad luck."

"Don't step on a crack or you'll break your mother's back."

"Spilling salt is a bad omen for things to come."

Maria had spent most of her childhood in perpetual worry that she would mess up. Do something careless that would ricochet its negative effects into all the years ahead of her. Or into her family's.

Just in case became her mantra, the worry beads her mind went to over and over again. Date rape? Better not go to the prom, just in case. Moving away after high school? College was a financial risk. Better to stay in her hometown. Get a stable but boring job, just in case she wasn't smart enough to handle something more challenging. Romantic relationships were fraught with unknowns. Better to stay single.

Maria rolled over on her side, drawing her knees up to her chest. She sighed. It was deep and heavy. "This trip is going to change your life," her therapist, Addie, had said. "Ecotherapy is a new practice to me too, but Dr. O'Dell is very familiar with it. He assures me that he's had clients who've undergone tremendous change in a short period of time. It's more popular in Europe, where counselors give clients prescriptions for time spent immersing themselves in nature. The results are astounding. You're going to break through barriers that would take us months of counseling sessions, Maria."

4

Now Maria looked at the alarm clocks by the bed. There were two: the one she used every morning—its annoying bleat familiar and hated—and a second one. A backup.

Just in case.

Clark Jenkins started cursing before opening his eyes. His head was pounding like a jackhammer on extra electrical current, his throat felt raw. His breath stank: a familiar brew of old cigarette smoke and sour gin. This time with an added hint of garlic.

What had he eaten for dinner? He focused on that detail. Easier to deal with than whatever had sent him on another bender. Bender. A stupid word to define getting drunk. What exactly was he bending? His opportunities?

He snorted and sat up in one motion.

Mistake.

The world spun one way and then another. He moaned for it to stop. Puking would make him feel better. Get the rest of this junk out of his system. But he didn't want to. He hated retching over the porcelain bowl, staring at the remains of the previous night. With his other hand he tentatively explored the pillow next to him.

The spinning got a tiny bit better when he found the other side of the bed empty. At least he hadn't brought Shelia or Beth home with him last night. Or anyone else. He couldn't deal with the nagging, the clutching at him, this early in the morning.

What time was it anyway? And what had woken him? Clark fumbled on the nightstand. The clock was blank, a little black bar where the numbers should be. He swore again, and checked his cell phone which he'd forgotten to plug in before he'd fallen into bed face first.

He walked to the kitchen, hand trailing his way on the wall.

Five after ten, the hands on the ugly gold face told him. What day? He leaned on the counter, willing the room to stop its orbit. Saturday. Saturday … Saturday … what was it he was supposed to do today? Coffee would help. His stomach burbled. Clark straightened and moved toward the pot. Then he remembered.

The trip. His counselor, Dr. O'Dell.

A string of curses rose to his lips. But the bile got there sooner. He bolted toward the bathroom.

Alaska Baines was running her heart out. At least, that's how it felt. It thumped and banged in her chest, begging her to stop, begging her to rest. What was that saying, *no rest for the wicked*? Then there was the other one, *no pain, no gain*, which pounded in her head along with the sound of her heartbeat.

Alaska was full of mantras; *try, try, try again*, and *only quitters quit*, and *there's no time like the present*. And more. Many, many more. She used mantras and sayings and proverbs and whatever else she could to motivate her team of junior ad executives. Rising to the top in the advertising department at the software firm and being a woman (doesn't being a woman always come in second?), Alaska needed all the help she could get.

It's why she did this. Running. She didn't even like it. But it served a greater purpose. Like so many things in her life—eating healthy, exercising like a mad woman, taking every personal and professional development seminar she could fit into her Type A, perfectly organized, color-coded schedule—it was necessary if she wanted to stay on top.

And Alaska did.

The trip this weekend would be a new experience for her. She'd been invited by her therapist to join the small group of clients that were going on an Ecotherapy weekend. Alaska had never been camping before, let alone backpacking. So of course, she'd said yes. It would be hard to be out of contact with work for a four-day weekend, but she'd made it work.

Feet slapping against the pavement, Alaska used a breathing technique her personal trainer had taught her to moderate her breathing. The stopwatch on her wrist told her she had three minutes to get to the mile marker if she was going to beat yesterday's record. She intended to.

Eyes on the prize. Focus, Alaska. Focus!

Gabe Southly moaned when his alarm clock went off, slapping at it with only one hand emerging from the cocoon of blankets. It was dark in there, and warm. He had no desire to emerge into the real world. While he drifted half-in and half-out of sleep he saw images. People from his past flitting across the screen of his mind, but in unusual ways. There was his favorite aunt, her lower body powerful horse's legs and she was riding a unicycle. And then the little dog they'd had as a family pet when Gabe was small appeared. It was dressed in a suit though, and when it turned its head to look at Gabe, it said, "Why do you think this is a good idea?" More images came, some humorous, some darker, all vivid.

It was this dream-wake stage that Gabe relished. That period between being completely conscious and still sleeping was when his creative mind flourished, feeding him images and ideas that were hard to capture in the rest of his busy day. Working as a freelance graphic designer wasn't at all what Gabe had pictured when he went to art school. No, he was going to be the one that stuck to his ideals, the purist who never dirtied his hand or his curriculum vitae with commercial art, who was never swayed by what a client wanted but only by his muse.

Gabe sighed and rubbed a hand over his face. His full consciousness was accompanied by the familiar tightness in his gut. The worries and fears always found their way to that spot and coagulated into a tight ball of stress and anxiety. Money, fame and fortune. Why was it that the things he wanted most seemed further out of reach every year?

He pushed himself up, out of the cocoon of blankets and checked the clock. He was meeting Alaska in just over an hour and still needed a shower and to finish packing his bag.

"This trip might just change your life," Dr. O'Dell had said.

Gabe had been seeing him for months now. Or was it more than a year? In fact, it was Gabe who had referred Alaska to his therapist. She was the one person he'd become friendly with at the tech company where he'd taken on some increasingly larger freelance graphic design jobs.

He yawned and pulled himself to standing. He didn't make friends, not easily, and he didn't want to let Alaska down. If nothing else, this weekend should cement the account with TriTech, something that would mean lots more business, and money, in his future.

Chapter Two

"Tell me again why you're going on this trip?" Adeline Preston's son, Ben, asked. Addie stopped shoving rolled up polypropylene clothes into her backpack. She looked at her youngest. He was handsome; dark hair and eyes like his father. The only trait of Addie's he'd inherited was his nose, straight and sprinkled with freckles. She hated her own dusting but on Ben they looked charming.

At twenty-three, *he* was charming, sweet. A worrier though, even since babyhood. Ben had always looked back to check for her permission: when he was learning to walk, when he was sampling his first solid foods. Not like Michael. Three years older and miles apart in personality, the boys had never gotten along. "The Swindler," she and her ex had nicknamed Michael when he was a toddler, because he always got what he wanted, one way or another.

"It's a group therapy session," Addie said and returned to stuffing. "Dr. O'Dell and I are leading the group. It's called Ecotherapy, a sort of immersion into the natural world. It's been used in Europe for a long time. It's effective," she grunted as she pushed the final piece of clothes into the too-tight bag. "And I get a chance to see Dell, I mean, Dr. O'Dell, in his own environment."

"He lives in the woods?" Ben's voice was sarcastic.

Addie looked up and smiled. "No, but he's spent enough time there to teach me a lot about nature."

"I could teach you anything you want to know about nature, Ma." Ben made a noise of disgust in the back of his throat. "You don't even like nature."

"That's not true." Addie turned to her son again. Looking up from the floor made him seem even taller. "I love nature."

"Wildlife shows on TV don't count," Ben said. He stuffed his hands into his pockets. His corduroys were oversized and his shirt hung out over the waistband, making him appear thicker around the waist than he was.

"Here, I got you this." He pulled something from the right-hand pocket and tossed it in her direction. Addie grabbed it right before it smacked her in the face. The object was thin, cylindrical and gold-colored. It looked like a fancy tube of lipstick but when her fingers moved to where the cap should be, there was only a tiny hole.

"Careful, it's pepper spray," Ben said. "Miniaturized. It'll fit easily into the pocket on your pants."

"Thanks, but isn't it a little small to stop a bear?"

"I got you a bigger version for that," he said, handing her another cylinder. This one was red and white and screamed "STOPS" along the side. In smaller print was a miniature bulleted list of all the animals the spray would halt in their

11

tracks: bears, snakes, wolves, mountain lions, panthers, coyotes, raccoons (!), humans.

"Raccoons? Should I be worried about those? I thought they were just greedy with leftovers." Addie laughed but Ben didn't join in.

"Rabies make any animal a danger," Ben said sounding like a professor. "The small one is for humans, just enough to surprise someone, give you a chance to get away." Ben had already reminded her several times of the attacks over the years on single women while hiking the Long Trail in the state. Addie had reminded him of the attacks that happened everywhere else. She was much more worried about animals than people.

"I'd feel better if you'd take this, too," Ben said, handing over a small pouch. It was heavier than it looked, with a nylon strap hanging from one end.

"What is it?"

"The stun gun. Look, I know you said—"

"No, Ben. Let's not talk about this again."

Ben crossed his arms, then let them hang loose, a sigh raising his shoulders up and down.

"Did you leave your itinerary somewhere?"

"Of course," she said, glad he wasn't going to start another argument about the stun gun. His concern would be sweet … if it wasn't so smothering. Instantly she felt badly for thinking like that. As a therapist, she knew the seriousness of anxiety, how it could choke a person's mind and smear their outlook with potential dangers.

While friends wouldn't define her as reckless, she'd

grown up in the '70s. It wasn't all peace, love and drugs; though she'd had her fair share of those. She'd done the typical college kid thing, taken a term off school to travel around Europe. Sometimes she cringed, thinking back to the dangerous situations she'd put herself into. She'd hitched rides from strangers, gotten tipsy in bars and one night had slept on a park bench in Berlin because she couldn't remember the name of her hotel. Ben would have a heart attack if he knew. But she had refused to live life like a caged animal. That's how the American dream always felt to her: white picket fence, a dog, and a car payment.

In the end wasn't it partially that—her refusal to accept the cage, to do things the way that was expected of her— that finally broke her marriage? Ben had so much of his father in him. Too much anxiety about all that could go wrong instead of grabbing the moments as they came and letting them be what they were without trying to control every second. But it was how he was wired. While she embraced change and trying new things, these made Ben uncomfortable. She'd always worked hard as a parent to recognize his strengths: he was very smart and excelled at working with computers and troubleshooting problems, something that Addie had no patience for. And he was tender-hearted, always standing up for the underdog. In fact, the one time he'd gotten in trouble for fighting at school had been when a bigger kid was picking on a younger, smaller child. She'd given him an ice cream cone and a hug after collecting him from school, rather than a lecture.

He cleared his throat and she looked up.

"Sorry," she said. "The itinerary is on the kitchen counter by the coffee pot. Don't worry about me, Ben," she tugged on Ben's pant leg and looked up at him. "Dr. O'Dell is very capable. We're going to be fine."

Butterflies tickled her ribs but she spread a wide smile over her face. She ducked her head, hoping Ben wouldn't see. She'd be lying if she said that Dr. O'Dell himself wasn't part of the reason she was so interested in this trip. For purely professional reasons, of course.

"What are your plans for the weekend?" she asked. "Are you getting together with Lacey?"

Ben shook his head, rubbed a hand on the back of his neck. "Nah. She's busy. Well, not busy really. Just doesn't want to see me." The last part of this was muffled as Ben's hand moved from the back of his head to rub the skin on his neck and face. He scrubbed at it vigorously, then let the hand drop.

"Oh, honey, I'm sorry. I didn't know that you were having problems."

"Yeah, me either."

"Do you want to talk about it?" Addie stood, stretching her back which was aching from the position hunched over her backpack. Her legs tingled.

"Not really," Ben said, shuffling his feet. "I've gotta run some errands. What time are you leaving?"

Addie glanced at her watch.

"Dr. O'Dell is picking me up in an hour." Not Dell as she'd been calling him for the past couple of months. Like he'd asked her to. Her cheeks were getting pink and Ben frowned. His dark eyes probing, lips already parting to ask a question.

One that Addie wouldn't want to answer.

"So, I'm almost done here. Sure you won't join me for a coffee and a chat about Lacey?"

Ben shook his head, breaking eye contact. Guilt twisted her gut. *What kind of mother uses her son's love life to avoid talking about her own?*

Chapter Three

Addie was pulling her backpack onto the porch, holding the screen door open with her rear end to wrestle the beast out of the house when Dell's truck pulled in. It was purple and green and looked like something you'd find at a tag sale in a church basement. Her backpack, not his truck.

Glancing up mid-heave, she smiled. The truck, like the man—and probably his backpack too—was sleek and perfectly kept. Her eyes followed his progress to the porch as she stretched out of the half-crouch to her feet.

What did he see as he walked toward her? The birdhouse pole on the far side of the driveway and the lamp post in need of fresh paint. A greenish color, split-level house that could use updated siding. Overgrown flower beds tangled after a season of healthy vigor. And when had those little mounds of dirt appeared on the lawn? Another mole, likely. Addie imagined that Dell's place was a minimalist's paradise, all sleek surfaces and bare of clutter.

"Need some help with that?" Dell asked chuckling.

"I think I've got it. Might need a little help getting it into your truck through. Lifting it higher than chest-height seems dangerous."

Dell's smile widened. "Here, let me," and yanked the pack upward, slinging it over his shoulder. If he hadn't staggered slightly, calf muscles bunching, Addie would have thought he was superhuman. She pulled the front door closed tight and double-checked the lock.

"All set?" he asked, retracing his path to the idling truck. Addie nodded even though he couldn't see her. She walked down the steps and felt the many bulging pockets on her shorts and windbreaker. Should the house key go into her pack or jacket pocket? The tiny zippered pocket over her hip or the one on the hiking vest? She'd probably forget where it was no matter where she put it.

"By nine the latest," she'd told Ben. Tuesday evening, home by nine p.m. That was the plan.

"I'll call you then," he'd replied, holding the itinerary she'd printed for him like the Holy Grail. "If you get back before, call me so I won't worry."

"I will, Ben," she'd said, hugging him hard.

"Did you forget the sink?" Dell asked now.

"What?"

"This bag weighs a ton." He grunted as he heaved the nylon pack into the rear of his truck. Addie peeked in and there was Dell's bag. Black and streamlined like she'd guessed, and no doubt perfectly packed. It had been years and years since Addie had toted her own backpack around Europe, and even then, she was constantly forgetting items behind in the hostels or leaving things behind on the train.

She'd laughed to friends made along the way that it was her calling card, how they would know she was ahead of them.

"I can help you repack it when we get to the trailhead if you want," Dell offered, walking toward the driver's side. Addie climbed in the passenger seat. The truck still had a new-car smell and was warm. There wasn't a hint of dust. No food wrappers, not even a stray hair.

"My son, Ben, insists that I will need everything in it at least once."

Dell raised his eyebrows.

"I'm concerned that you won't make it more than a mile, hauling that thing." Dell glanced at her for a moment before shifting the truck into reverse. Addie's cheeks warmed. Was he trying to tell her inadvertently that she was out of shape? She was, but still. While she managed to keep her weight down, she didn't embark on any of the long walks or ski trips that she'd loved in her younger years. And her thighs and biceps reminded her of this on a regular basis.

Addie turned her head, looking at Dell's profile. His eyes were dark brown and the lashes behind his round glasses were thick and dark. He had a slightly narrow face, but it lent an air of professor-ness to him. Full lips. It was odd seeing him in outdoor clothes, though. She'd grown used to the ties and vests and carefully pressed dress pants he wore at work.

"You're probably right," she said. "Taking a look at the pack before we go is a good idea."

He backed out and she caught a lemony-pine scent. His aftershave was enticing in the office and smelled even better here, in the enclosed space. She looked out the window, trying to clear her mind. A crush on your boss is no big deal, if he doesn't know about it. Other than the discomfort it causes, of course.

"There are mini versions of the clients' files in that accordion file behind your seat," he said. "If you want a refresher."

"Thanks." Addie stretched, seatbelt pulling at her neck and grabbed the folder, flipping through the contents.

She and Dell had been talking about the trip and the clients who would be coming for weeks now, over coffee at work, and once over lunch at *Chantal's*, a beautiful little French restaurant in town. Four clients were attending the long-weekend trip. Only one was Addie's own, Maria Rodriguez. The others were Dell's: two men and another woman. "Like a triple date," Addie had nearly blurted out when Dell had first approached her with the idea. She'd stopped herself, thank God, realizing how unprofessional the joke would be.

As the newest counselor at Maplehurst Mental Health— M&M everyone called it— she was very conscious of her status as greenhorn. "You're a natural," Dell had told her more than once, but still, Addie worried that she wouldn't fit in with the other, more experienced counselors. She'd been grateful Dell had asked her to be part of this trip. Surprised, but grateful.

"Do you have any backpacking experience?" he'd asked her then, leaning on his desk. Addie had sat in a low chair near the gas fireplace, watching Dell watch her. The clock on the wall behind her ticked loudly.

"I used to bring my boys backpacking when they were

young. We did a few overnighters, but it's been a long time."

"It's like riding a bicycle," Dell had said. "It will all come back to you. Besides, the time in nature will do you good."

Addie had smiled and nodded.

It would also be great to get back into the woods. It had been too long, Dell was right. Finishing first her bachelor's and then her graduate degree as an adult student hadn't been easy. The last few years of school had stretched out even longer because she'd been working full-time between classes and papers and hours of clinical work. After she'd graduated and started working it was hard to plan hiking trips. Even weekend ones when the boys were small, felt overwhelming.

Besides, she'd needed the weekends to catch up: running errands, doing all the housework that never got done during the week. Kenneth, her ex-husband, was no help in that area. He spent most of his weekends schmoozing with prospective clients on the golf course, or flying across the country to lead sales trainings.

The file in Addie's hand tipped and the contents began to spill onto her lap. She shook herself mentally and glanced at Dell. He looked straight ahead at the road, a slight smile on his lips, humming along with a Neil Diamond song on the radio. Her palms felt a little damp against the files. She flipped open the first: a woman named Alaska Baines, mid-forties, career in PR at a tech company that Addie recognized as one of the biggest in the area. "Stress management," read Dell's neat notes under the focus of treatment area. "Reduction?" he'd noted with a question mark underneath.

The second file belonged to a man named Gabe Southly,

an artist and poet who'd sought out counseling for "creative block." His file too, noted "anxiety issues" under the treatment area. Clark Jenkins was the name on the third file and Addie was surprised to see the diagnosis of anger management. She'd naturally assumed that a group session would be more effective if the clients shared similar treatment plans.

"This client, Clark," Addie said, holding a finger near the small box on the chart. "His diagnosis is the only one that's not in the realm of stress and anxiety." She looked at Dell who flashed her a smile. The wide pink lips showed white teeth beneath.

"True. Not anxious on the surface at least, but I've been working with him for some time. Although his treatment plan is for anger management and the challenging way he deals with it, underneath the frustration and rage, I sense a deep fear. You know that old saying: all humans feel only two emotions: fear and love."

"Hmm?" Addie put the file down on her lap and turned in her seat toward Dell.

"The base of every human emotion is either fear or love: hate is fueled by fear. Jealousy is fueled by fear. Compassion is fueled by love. Generosity can be fueled by either."

"Either?" Addie asked. "Generosity doesn't come from fear."

"I believe it does," Dell said, turning on the left blinker and slowing at a stop sign. "There are millionaires who give tons of money away, not out of the goodness of their hearts but because of tax breaks and loop holes and the desire, deep down—maybe even an unconscious level—to get more. They give to get."

"That's a little cynical, isn't it?"

Dell looked over at her and smiled. Her heart thumped a little harder than Addie thought necessary.

"I think like a realist," he said.

Addie looked down, flipped through the rest of Clark's chart. "So you are treating him as though he has anxiety issues, rather than anger issues?" It was an interesting concept. One she hadn't heard of before. But then there were a lot of Dell's treatment methods that were more innovative than others she'd known. Take this trip for instance. Ecotherapy wasn't new to the world of psychology, but it still wasn't mainstream by any means.

"I think it will be effective," he replied.

She read in silence for several more minutes, before the swaying of the truck on the back roads made her stomach roil. Finally, she tucked the files back where they came from and pressed her hands together between her knees.

Dell looked over at her and then back toward the road, expertly avoiding a pothole.

"Tell me … son of a—" His hands gripped the steering wheel as though he were trying to snap it in half.

At first, Addie didn't know what was wrong. She looked at him, about to ask when she saw it. An eighteen-wheeler had drifted over the yellow dashed lines and was headed straight toward them.

Dell slammed one hand on the horn and held it there. He swerved to the right, dangerously close to the edge of a road fringed with bent and rusted guardrails. Addie's right hand scrabbled for the door handle, her left clawed at the leather seat. A scream sat behind her lips. She pulled her eyes away from the semi-trailer long enough to see the bottom of the ravine below the guardrails, far, far away.

Chapter Four

The trucker either heard Dell's horn or roused himself from his stupor just before ramming into the pickup. The big truck lumbered back over to its own side of the road. Dell swore and Addie glanced at it just in time to see a frightened, very white face hovering over the big steering wheel of the semi. She hadn't uttered a sound, not a single peep, but her fingers were molded into the soft leather of the truck's passenger seat.

"Are you all right?" Dell asked. "That was close."

"I ..." Addie tried to respond but no other words came. Dell slowed, but didn't stop the pickup. There was no room, no shoulder to speak of on the narrow road. They rode slowly and silently for several long minutes.

"That was ... terrifying," Addie said, finally. For some reason the words made her laugh. Or maybe it was leftover hysteria. Dell glanced at her and chuckled, as she erupted into full belly laughs. Finally, she got a handle on her emotion, wiped her eyes and leaned her head back on the seat rest.

"Sorry. I'm not sure where that came from."

"A normal response to excessive stress," Dell said. "Most people either laugh or cry."

"Be grateful I have a sense of humor," Addie said.

It was quiet another couple of minutes and then Dell said, "I was going to ask you, earlier, to tell me a little bit more about you. I know only your professional side. And that you have two grown sons. But what do you like to do in your free time, Adeline? What do you fill your hours with outside the office?"

She was about to say, "Call me Addie, please," but didn't. She'd asked him twice already to use her nickname, but he either didn't remember or didn't care for it. She leaned back in her seat a bit. The question felt momentous: what did she like doing in her free time?

"I like the arts: going to theater shows and art openings. And outdoor things: hiking and biking and gardening."

Briefly images of her boys' childhood filled her mind. Teaching them to juggle and walk on a tightrope (a nylon strap held up between two posts). Her ex asking her more than once if she was training them for the circus. They'd spent hours at the frog pond catching and releasing all manner of slimy things. Nights out under the stars, absorbing the whole, big world in glittering breaths. The boys had loved it. She missed those days. When being natural and playful and *herself*, hadn't been so difficult.

How long had it been since Addie had actually been to the theater? Out camping or hiking? Gardening was the one leftover hobby, more habit than desire. The thought of the big garden beds standing empty all summer, or worse, growing over with weeds made her get out her hoe and seed packets in early spring every year.

"What about you?" Addie asked, trying to fill in the too-long silence. "I know you enjoy hiking and overnight camping. Anything else?"

Dell nodded. "Rock climbing, ice climbing in the winter months. And distance running. Basically anything that has to do with fresh air and getting sweaty." He smiled and turned toward her for a second. His dark eyes were lined so thickly with lashes that they looked fake. She felt a little lurch in her gut, swallowed and nodded, turning to look out her window. The truck was smooth on the pavement, the air in the cab too warm.

A few minutes later they passed through a small town with the typical squat buildings: two gas stations, a church, a quick mart with a tiny post office attached to its side and a small brick library. Shortly after, they bounced into a pockmarked parking lot. She recognized the bright green sign and the annoying mascot peeking over the edge of the car rental facility. The lot was nearly empty, most of the rentals were parked behind the building. Dell parked the pickup and hopped out.

"I've reserved the van online so it should be just a few minutes," he said and jogged toward the building. A few sprinkles dotted the windshield. She surveyed the parking lot through the drops, looking for the clients joining their group. There was Maria, in an older model Ford sedan across the lot.

The air was cooler here than at home, the clouds had

crowded the sunshine and a chilly breeze nipped at her cheeks and hands as Addie got out of the truck and headed toward Maria.

"Hi," she called, waving. But Maria was looking down in her lap. Addie got closer and knocked gently on the driver side window. "Good morning, Maria."

Inside the car Maria jumped, the cell phone in her hands flying onto the floor at her feet. She said something that Addie couldn't hear then scrambled for the phone and simultaneously opened the door a crack.

"I'm sorry, I didn't see you," Maria said.

"That's all right. I called out but I guess you didn't hear me. Are you ready for this adventure?" Addie scanned the back seat and saw two packs, big and lumpy. "Are those both yours?"

Maria nodded, her face looked guilty. "I wanted to be sure I had enough of everything."

Addie laughed. "Me too. I think De … Dr. O'Dell will have to sort us out before we leave the parking lot at the trail."

Maria smiled. She was beautiful, magazine quality perfect except for a thin winding scar that led from her eyebrow to mid-cheek. Addie never asked about it and Maria had never volunteered any information.

"Is everyone else here?" Maria asked, getting out from behind the wheel and scanning the parking lot. Addie held the door open further.

"I'm not sure. I don't know the others. They're clients of Dr. O'Dell's."

"Oh," Maria said. "I feel like it's the first day of school or something."

"I know. I'm feeling the same way. We're outside of our comfort zones so it's to be expected, right?"

"I guess," Maria said. She sighed and looked around the lot. "Where is he? Dr. O'Dell?"

"Getting the van. He shouldn't be long."

Dell strode out of the door at that moment, layers of expensive hiking clothes making a *swish swish* sound as he walked. He paused, then glanced in their direction and walked over.

"All set," he said, holding up a key on a ring that also held a big green keychain. He surveyed the parking lot briefly.

"Ah. There are Alaska and Gabe, I see," he nodded toward a posh Audi SUV. The two waved and opened the vehicle's doors simultaneously.

"They know each other?" Maria asked, her voice trembling. Addie patted the woman's arm. The only thing worse than the first day of school is when everyone else already knows each other.

"Yes, Gabe does some freelance artwork for the company where Alaska works," Dell said. "I don't see Clark yet, but we'll go ahead and start loading the van. He'll be here shortly, I'm sure."

Dell jogged over to give the same instructions to Gabe and Alaska while Maria turned toward the car, biting her lip.

"I think this was a mistake," she said. A flush of red spread up her neck from her T-shirt. "I don't want to go." These last words were said so quietly that Addie almost missed them. She put a hand on Maria's shoulder.

"I know that this is uncomfortable," she said. "We have to move through the discomfort of doing scary things though, in order to reap the benefits and rewards it will bring. Tell me what you're feeling right now, the thoughts going through your head."

"Scared. Nearly panicked. I don't want to do this. This was a stupid idea. I don't even like nature. I hate being around strangers and this is going to be so much worse in close quarters. I can't get away. I can't escape …" her voice trailed off and Addie saw the young woman's shoulders start to hitch quickly up and down. She wasn't crying but was having trouble breathing. She'd struggled with panic attacks, though as far as Addie knew she hadn't had one in months.

"Maria, you are going to be fine. I'm right here with you. Nothing bad is going to happen to you. Take one deep breath. No, deeper. Good. Hold it for a count of three: one … two … three. Excellent. And now let it out, slowly. Slowly. Another one in: one … two … three. Very good. And out slowly. Great.

"Continue with that, deep breath in for three and then hold. And then let it out, slowly. Listen to my voice, Maria, as you continue to breathe. Just listen. You are a brave woman and you are more than capable of facing your fear. That's what this trip is giving you the opportunity to do. To set some boundaries with that fear. It does not control you." Addie paused for a deeper breath of her own.

"Every step that you take on this trip, from here on out, is a step closer to where you most want to be. Every fear that pops up—and there will be plenty—you have the power inside of you to deal with." After a moment, she continued. "Good job with the breathing. I can see your body is more relaxed."

And it was. Maria's shoulders had lowered, the breaths helping her to regain equilibrium. Even the rash had faded from bright red to pink.

"Now, can you tell me how you're feeling? Take your time, there is no rush."

Maria was quiet for several long seconds, then, "Better. Still scared but the panic is gone. I know that I need to do what we've been talking about: focus on just one fear at a time, one step at a time. It's when I let the fear run rampant that the panic sets in."

"Great. And yes, that's a wonderful reminder you've given yourself."

Maria took several more deep breaths and then turned and looked at Addie.

"Thank you. That could have gotten really ugly."

Addie smiled. "And it may still. At some point, you may have another full-on attack like you used to. But I'm confident now that you know what to do. I helped you through this one but I wasn't doing anything that you aren't fully capable of doing for yourself. You've grown so much in these past few months, Maria. Can you see that?"

"Sometimes," Maria said. "Maybe not so much right now."

Addie laughed and patted her shoulder. "You have. Whether you see it or not. You are continuing to grow and stretch and do brave things that didn't seem possible just months ago. Now," Addie looked toward the van. "Can I help you with your packs?"

Addie had barely finished asking when a jacked up pickup truck roared into the parking lot, tires squealing.

Maria gasped. Addie's heart jumped into her esophagus. She looked wildly toward Dell who was standing directly in the path of the truck. Then a sharp crack, like the retort of a gun, came from the vehicle.

Addie and Maria both dropped to the side of the car, frozen like rabbits. The truck's engine cut out and the door opened and slammed shut. Fingers trembling, Addie peeked over the side of the door. Through the glass she saw a man striding from the vehicle straight toward Dell and his two clients.

Do something. He's going to kill him! Her breath was coming in shallow gasps and her limbs weren't cooperating. The man drew closer. He said something and waved his hands but the sound of a delivery truck downshifting on the road nearby drowned out the words.

Maria was crouched near the car, eyes closed, swaying slightly.

"I'll be right back. Don't move," Addie said to the younger woman. She crossed the lot, staying to the left of the angry-looking man. His right hand was empty, gesturing toward the truck and then the road but she couldn't see his left. Was the gun there? She stayed in what she hoped was in the man's blind spot. Her own left hand fumbled with the zipper of her jacket where she'd tucked her cell phone.

"… which is when all hell broke loose," the man was saying. "… tried to call but …" Again the words too hard to hear, taken away by the wind that had picked up.

"It's not a problem, Clark," Dell said soothingly. "We're all still here, still in the process of loading the van. You got here in time. It sounds like you've had quite a morning, though."

Dell's third patient? She checked the man's left hand. It was empty. So what was that explosion a few minutes ago?

Addie felt a wave of embarrassment wash over her. Here she was acting like a scared rabbit Instead of one of the leaders in charge. She cleared her throat, walked the last few steps to join the small group.

"Clark?" she held out her hand. It was shaking slightly. "I'm Addie Preston, the other counselor leading the group." The man turned, his face too-red in the chilly air. He glanced at her hand for a second, then shook it. His own was calloused, dry. He nodded in response, his mouth turned into something of a smile but his eyes didn't crinkle around the edges.

"And you must be Alaska and Gabe," she said, turning to the other two. Alaska was tall and fit looking, one of those women who looks like an ad for athletic apparel anytime you see them running. Gabe was tall and thin, too, though he looked more like someone who stayed slim by smoking too many cigarettes. He'd nervously run a hand over his head to smooth down baby fine hair before shaking her hand. She turned and shook Alaska's.

"Nice meeting you," Alaska said, her gaze skimming Addie from head to foot before dropping her hand. "Dr. O'Dell, are we going to get the van loaded? It looks like rain."

Dell made an approving noise and nodded toward the van, then turned back to Clark. Quietly, so quietly that Addie nearly didn't hear him, the psychologist said, "How's that new medicine working out for you?"

She couldn't hear the big man's response but waited until Dell had jogged ahead to unlock the back doors of the van and fell in line with Clark.

"What was that noise when you drove in? I thought someone was shooting up the parking lot," she laughed when she said it, holding her still wobbly hands together to keep them from giving her away.

"Backfire. My truck needs a tune up bad, but I've been working a lot of overtime and haven't had time to work on it." He climbed in the truck. "Better move it," he said. Addie thought he was talking to her, then realized he meant the truck, which was blocking the entrance. "Been a rotten morning," he said, as he put the truck into first gear. "Hope the rest of the trip turns out better."

Chapter Five

Dr. David O'Dell steered the van over some loose dirt and gravel and onto the pull off. The trailhead was just above them, one he'd climbed before. It wasn't exactly a beginner trail, not the way he'd described it to the group, even to Adeline, but he was confident they'd all be fine.

People's minds restricted them far more than their physical capabilities. He'd learned that early on. If you told someone they were about to do something hard, something that would challenge them in new ways, most would avoid the task. But if they simply began, unsure of how difficult a process or new experience was, well, that's when real and positive change happened.

He cut the engine. Alaska and Gabe stopped chatting about graphics and website analytics long enough to peer out the window. A dark canopy of trees covered most of the parking area. There were no other vehicles. October was the perfect time in Vermont to hike, though this was later in the season than was ideal. It had been the only weekend available though, a conference taking a lot of Dell's time earlier in the month. It would be fine. The weather forecast was for mostly sunny skies and he was looking forward to the new challenge of leading a group of clients on an outdoor therapy weekend. He'd been intrigued by the idea since he first heard about a psychiatrist here in the New England area who led groups like this infrequently. This would be a sort of pilot program. Dell already had some tentative dates in mind for the next hiking season.

"So," Dell said, unbuckling his belt and turning to make eye contact. "Are we ready to really experience all that nature has to offer this weekend?"

If he'd been waiting for a rousing cheer, he'd have been disappointed. Gabe and Alaska smiled in response, Clark was glaring at the window, and Adeline's client, Maria, stared at the hands in her lap. Folding and refolding them over and over again.

"Sure," said Addie, filling in the awkward pause. "Right, everyone?" she said. There was even less response from the group. She turned to Dell.

"Should we get our packs out now?"

"Let's go over a few basics first. Out of the van, everyone. Let's stretch our legs and get some fresh air."

The van doors squawked open and the group emerged, blinking into the suddenly sun-filled air. There were no raindrops here, though signs of recent rain were apparent. The logs bordering the parking lot—makeshift seats—were damp and the leaves on bushes and trees sagged slightly with moisture.

"All right," Dell said. "The first thing we're going to talk about is safety in the woods." Clark snorted quietly but Dell ignored him. He told the group about what to do and not to do if approached by wild animals, gave a five-minute demonstration on emergency first aid, adding in that "you'll likely never need to know this," when he saw how pale Maria's face was. He told them about exposure and sleeping in the great outdoors. Finally, he went over his pack with them, showing them all the essentials that had been on the packing list given out weeks ago.

"I'm going to be right here with you, along with Dr. Preston," Dell said. He felt rather than saw Adeline jerk in surprise to his left. "So there's really nothing to worry about. All of this instruction is just a precaution, in the chance you were to become separated from the group." He handed out stapled pages next, maps of the area they were to hike.

"Cell phone service is slim to nil this far out, so trusting the GPS on your phone won't work. Everyone has a compass, correct?"

Nods all around.

"Do you each know how to use it?"

Nods again, some less certain than others. "We can go over that again tonight. It will give us something to do around the campfire." He smiled. "Any questions?"

No one spoke.

"Very good. Then let's get our packs out first. Dr. Preston and Maria, let's take a closer look at yours and see if we can whittle them down for easier carrying. Anyone else who feels that their pack is too heavy or is concerned that it could be packed more efficiently, please join us."

Clark sighed, deep and loud. "What are the rest of us supposed to do?"

Dell smiled over his shoulder. "Be patient. Explore. Rest. It's going to be a long time before you sit down again."

Twenty-five minutes later, the group was moving. A mixture of trepidation and excitement bubbled in Addie's chest. Dell had told her it would be best if she fell back, brought up the rear. Instead she jogged to catch up to him.

"Why did you call me Dr. Preston?" she asked. Already her breath was coming hard.

Dell slowed slightly. "The title gives a certain confidence. I figure that our group can use that right now."

Addie considered that.

"Do you object?" Dell asked. He smiled at her but the words were tinged with sarcasm. Or was she imagining that?

"No, of course not. It's fine."

"Good. Now, if you don't mind following up the rear, just to make sure we don't lose anyone—"

"Right," Addie said and pulled off to the side of the trail, letting the rest of the group pass by.

She was about to fall into line behind Maria when she saw movement in the bushes. A squirrel probably, gathering nuts. It was loud, scuttling through the underbrush. Addie turned, reached for the handkerchief on the waist belt of her pack. Her face was moist with sweat already. Or was it mist? The sun had fallen behind some clouds overhead. Darkening clouds, she noted.

She saw movement from the corner of her eye. The

sounds in the underbrush grew louder. She looked toward the sound, expecting a squirrel or two to emerge. Instead she saw a face. Dark, with golden-colored eyes. It looked out from the bushes about the height of Addie's waist. Addie's breath tangled in her throat and a sound that was half moan, half-surprise came out. A hand went to her mouth, automatically. She closed her eyes, opened them again.

And it was gone.

She looked again and again, searching the bushes and tree trunks, peering far to the right and left of where the face had been, looking for movement of any kind.

Nothing.

"Are you coming?" a voice called out.

Addie jumped.

Maria stood on the trail yards ahead of her, swaying slightly under the still-heavy pack.

"Yes," Addie said. "Right behind you."

"Is everything alright?" Maria asked when Addie caught up. "You look like you've seen a ghost."

Could she confide in Maria, tell her what she'd seen? Her brain scrambled to categorize it. A bear? A mountain lion? Did those even live in Vermont? But what she'd seen was too much like a person. Or an ape. She wiped the handkerchief across her forehead, then knotted it around her neck like a bandit.

"I'm fine. Just a touch of dizziness. Must have been the ride up here. Go ahead," Addie said, waving toward the trail. "We don't want to get left behind."

Chapter Six

Whooo, whooo. Whooo? The campfire snapped, sending sparks into an upward cascade. The owl hooted again, or maybe it was a second one, Gabe couldn't be sure. He glanced around the circle of faces, studying them in the firelight. It was interesting how the light and shadows dancing on the planes of faces changed them so much. He wished he could draw Dr. Preston right now. She sat directly across from him, staring unseeing into the fire.

She was an attractive woman: long auburn hair with just a little gray starting to show, dark eyes and good cheekbones with a splatter of freckles across them and the bridge of her nose. Not beautiful, not striking. She'd probably never been called a sexpot or Siren even in her younger days. Yet there was an air of sensuality around her. What did the French call it? A *je ne sais quoi*. Something you couldn't put a finger on. Self-assurance, maybe. Comfort in her own skin.

Dr. O'Dell walked over to the campfire, interrupting Gabe's musing. All eyes looked up at him. Alaska smiled, stretching her long, tanned neck back, pushing her chest forward. Alaska and Dr. O'Dell? He'd seen stranger pairings. But Dr. O'Dell wasn't looking at Alaska. His eyes were on Dr. Preston.

The therapist cleared his throat. "Has anyone seen a small, black nylon bag, about so big?" Dr. O'Dell held out his hands approximately eight inches apart. "It's missing from my pack." People all around the fire shook their heads. His eyes fell on Gabe last.

"No," Gabe said. "Sorry, I haven't."

Dr. O'Dell smiled and sighed, then retraced his path back to the sleek tent he'd put up. The three women had claimed the small cabin at the campsite. First come first served when you're hiking. The men had spread their tents around the outskirts of the campsite—if that's what you called a relatively flat piece of ground in the middle of nowhere. This was unlike any camping Gabe had ever done. His grandparents, who he'd lived with, considered the weekend that their RV's air conditioner broke roughing it.

The others had returned to staring into the fire. It was mesmerizing, almost hypnotic. Gabe studied them a few minutes more, watching them watch the fire. Then he got to his feet, languidly.

"Guess I'll turn in," he said. "I'm beat."

"Goodnight, Gabe," Dr. Preston said.

"Goodnight," the other women chorused at the same time.

Clark was already rooting around in his own tent, when Gabe walked past. The big man was swearing from time to time between the whispers of nylon on nylon.

Gabe stretched and yawned, head thrown back and looked up at the sky. The dark clouds from earlier were still there, blocking out the stars and moon. A light wind rattled the fabric of his tent and he shivered suddenly, then unzipped the tent and climbed inside, making sure to leave his shoes outside. Bad enough the tent was on the dirt, it didn't need to be inside too.

He spent a few minutes settling in, then turned his collapsible lantern on low and put it by his head. He propped a book on his chest and turned halfway in his sleeping bag, feeling underneath the pillow. There it was. He patted the small nylon bag. He hadn't thought Dr. O'Dell would realize it was missing so soon. No matter. The good doctor would have other things to keep him safe. He was the great outdoorsman, right? The gun, tucked in its small nylon case made Gabe feel better, more secure.

How long would Dr. O'Dell look for it? He smiled, opened his book and started to read.

Alaska waited until the other two women had retreated to the cabin before dousing the fire. She scooped handfuls of dirt onto it, then when the fire didn't die fast enough, used her hiking boot to drag more earth over the embers.

She sighed, looked up at the sky. A couple of the brightest stars shone through the dark blanket of clouds overhead. The wind was picking up and moving the clouds around, darker smears of black moving over the navy-blue sky.

She was tired; a different kind of fatigue than she was

used to. At the end of most workdays, which usually fell within the hours of eleven and midnight, her brain was exhausted. A mix of too much caffeine, too much time online, too many fires being put out. She went to bed most nights feeling jumpy only to have dreams she was running from some dark thing she couldn't see.

This fatigue was different. A pleasant mix of body aches and exposure to fresh air. Her brain felt, strangely, rested. Odd since it hadn't stopped worrying about work the entire day. But the responsibility was gone. She couldn't do anything to help now, not from here in the middle of nowhere. There was liberation in that.

Alaska bit her lip and glanced in the very dim light from a partially covered half-moon toward David's tent. A light breeze shook the corners. She imagined what it would be like to slip out of her clothes and into the interior. What would his reaction be? She knew he wanted her, had known it since their very first visit nearly a year ago. In truth, she hadn't needed to continue the visits past the first two months. She'd gone to him hurting, in pain after the death of her mother. But that pain had long subsided. Or at least dulled to a bearable ache.

Alaska smiled. The anxiety issue had been created to continue the visits. David wasn't yet at a point where he could see how perfect they were together, not quite ready to give her up as a patient to pursue something deeper and more meaningful. But he would. He just needed a little more time.

Isn't that why he'd asked her if she wanted to join this

trip? Finally, they would have time together outside of his office. This weekend would be the impetus to change their relationship forever, to finally take things to the next level.

She turned and walked toward the cabin. The night air was still, other than the sound of leaves in the canopy overhead, whispering together. Then a crack. A stick breaking nearby? A branch splitting? Alaska's eyes searched the woods where the sound had come from. She saw nothing.

Standing motionless, she waited. Her hands went to her pockets but she'd left her flashlight in the cabin. Stupid mistake. She walked in the direction the noise came from. If it were an animal it would be best to frighten it away from camp, wouldn't it? Footsteps nearly noiseless, Alaska crept toward the line of trees.

There it was again, this time a little closer to their campsite. There was a rustle of leaves. Definitely an animal of some kind. She was at the edge of the woods now but walked no further. What good could she do in the dark without any weapon? Besides, it could be a skunk.

She waited another few minutes, stood stalk still in the silence. No sound, no noises other than an occasional creak or groan from the trees and the far-away call of an owl eternally asking the same question.

Finally she turned, walked back to the cabin. Opening the door, she glanced one more time toward the woods.

And then she screamed.

Chapter Seven

"I know what I saw," Alaska's voice sounded high and hysterical even in her own ears. She took a deep breath, tried to slow her breathing, slow the pulse skittering in her wrists.

"I believe you, Alaska," David's voice was gentle, reassuring. "You saw an animal and no one is questioning—"

"It wasn't just any animal. It wasn't a cute fluffy bunny out there, or an opossum family nibbling crumbs off the ground. This was a ... a ..." Her voice lost steam. She rubbed a hand over her face angrily. *Ridiculous.*

"I know what I saw," she repeated. *No, you don't.*

A loud, dry chuckle that sounded like metal against metal came from Clark. "Sure, we believe you. Big Foot is real and you saw him trucking around in the woods. Was he trying to get into Dr. O'Dell's tent? Maybe it was a lady Big Foot, wanting to get lucky."

Alaska glared at him. Her fists were in tight coils near her legs. "You didn't see it. That face—"

"You didn't see it either," Clark interrupted. "You were probably sleepwalking."

"I was not sleepwalking, you idiot! I hadn't even gone into the cabin yet."

"Well there's no way that you could see anything out here. It's black as tar." Clark shook his head and turned to walk back to his tent. He muttered something under his breath that sounded suspiciously like, "stupid female."

"Alaska," David was speaking to her again. "I believe you. You saw something in the woods, something that startled you. But sometimes our eyes, our minds, play tricks on us." He continued on despite her weak protests. "Is there any chance that what you saw was, well, on all fours?"

"No. I told you already. It was right there," she pointed toward the spot where she'd seen the face. She shivered, remembering those eyes. Almost golden in the dim light. As though they were glowing.

"Bobcats are prevalent here. There have even been supposed sightings of catamounts, or mountain lions as they're known in the west. I don't necessarily believe that myself, but bears are a common—"

"It wasn't a bear. I've never seen a bobcat but I don't think …" Alaska sighed, rubbed her hands over her arms. Was that what it was? A big cat, maybe stretched with its legs on a tree to scratch it. Did they do that? Heat remained in her cheeks. She felt small and stupid, like when her father used to point out the single error on a test she'd brought home, asking her in a condescending tone how she couldn't have known that.

Her skin tingled. "Maybe you're right and it wasn't … wasn't what I thought."

"Come and rest, Alaska," this was Dr. Preston speaking, her voice low and comforting. Did she save this voice for especially crazy patients? Alaska wanted to laugh, wanted to blurt out, "I'm not crazy! I just want to see David every week." But she didn't. She wanted to turn and fling herself into David's arms, hear his strong heartbeat and feel warmth in the circle of his arms. Instead, she just turned and walked toward the cabin, hunching her shoulders and rubbing her hands up and down her arms. She'd expected Dr. Preston to fall into step with her. Instead she heard the low murmuring voices: hers and David's together. Comparing notes? Categorizing her symptoms? Laughing to themselves?

The door of the cabin creaked a little when she pushed through it. Maria was tucked so deeply into her sleeping bag that Alaska couldn't see anything but a lump beneath the puffy fabric. How did someone sleep through all of that?

Alaska took her shoes off and slid into her own down bag completely clothed. Behind her lids she saw the golden eyes. It will take hours to fall asleep now, she thought. But minutes later she felt her body drifting and then sleep pulled her under.

"What do you think it really was?" Addie asked Dell.

"Bobcats are out year-round and the golden eyes that she mentioned would fit. It could have been up high, on a branch, making it appear that it was standing. Whatever it was, I'm sure it was scared out of its wits and won't be back tonight," he motioned toward the cabin. "You should get some sleep. We'll have to break camp early tomorrow if

46

we're going to make it to Shiny Creek before dark."

Addie nodded but didn't move. Should she tell him what she saw earlier? That she too had seen the glowing eyes Alaska had mentioned?

"Goodnight," he said after a few seconds, moving toward his tent. "And, Adeline?"

She looked up at him. His hair was slightly askew, glasses glinting in the pale moonlight.

"Try not to worry."

Addie tossed in her sleeping bag for over an hour. She knew because every several minutes she'd press the night light on her sports watch, looking at the numbers that were moving like molasses. She rolled from one side to the other, trying to find a comfortable position, trying to block out the image of those eyes …

"Addie?" a soft voice asked, shaking her shoulder gently.

Moaning, Addie threw an arm over her face and asked, "What is it?"

"We have to break camp soon. Dr. O'Dell said to let you sleep as long as possible but if you want any hot water you have to get up now. They're putting the stove away."

Addie scrunched down further in her sleeping bag, pulling it over her head. An image of a piping hot cup of coffee, even instant coffee, made her rethink her actions. She sighed and shoved the bag away.

"Thanks, Maria. I'll be right out."

"OK."

Addie heard the cabin door squeak shut. She rubbed her hands over her face. It took a few long seconds to reorient herself to the layout of the little room. Bunks lined two walls, space for four to sleep comfortably stacked on top of each other. She wouldn't use the term "bunk bed," because there were no mattresses. Just platforms made of wood. Campers over the years had carved initials and short, choppy messages into the wood of the walls and the upper bunks using jackknives. "B.R. was here, 2001," and "Rottie + Jeanboy, 1998" and more like these.

They'd turned in so late last night she hadn't even gotten a chance to read the logbook. All cabins and lean-tos on the Long Trail had them, a written record of backpackers traveling through. Addie had always enjoyed reading the entries and seeing the trail names that people picked for themselves.

The logbook had a more important purpose, of course. It also served as a safety record. If anyone went missing, the logbook helped authorities to determine the course that the person had traveled, narrowing down the search area.

Addie stood slowly. The air in the little structure was freezing. She found the logbook tucked into a little alcove near the front door. She grabbed it, then jumped back into her still-warm sleeping bag. Coffee would be welcome but she could always make some when the group stopped for lunch. She didn't want to miss out on reading through the last few entries and adding her own. What had her trail name been when the boys were little? She couldn't remember, and anyway, it was time for a new one.

Thumbing through the pages, Addie came to the two pages of most recent entries. She skimmed them, reading quickly. The air was so cold, Addie was surprised she couldn't see her breath.

"Made camp just after sunset," an entry last week read. "Beautiful day for a hike. Weather in the mid-sixties and sunny. I love Vermont!"

And another, "Skinny Minnie and me stayed at cabin for two days. Bad weather, storm passed through. Letting up today, heading back on the trail."

Addie scanned through the earlier pages, then let out a breath. Was it frustration or relief she felt in her chest? No mention of strange beasts with glowing, golden eyes. Had she really expected that? She tugged the pencil free from the notebook's spiral binding and unknotted the gray string wondering what to write.

"Beautiful weather for our group hike. Looking forward to more of the same as we push to Shiny Creek tonight. Saw an animal last night … bobcat?" The pencil in her hand shook slightly. Addie stared at the logbook, trying to think of a good trail name for herself. Backpack Mama? Redheaded Stepchild? She snorted. She needed something else, something that felt independent and self-reliant. Even if that's not exactly how she was feeling on this trip.

Fearful Flyer, she scrawled. It fit. Fearful because she was in a place that was stretching her, making her uncomfortable. And flyer because she was going out and doing it, taking risks and seeing what happened. She liked it.

She pushed the bag away and stood up. Immediately goosebumps ran up and down her arms and legs. If she hurried to pull on her second layer, maybe she could still get some of that hot water before they tossed it.

Addie reached under the bottom bunk for her backpack. She could practically feel the warmer layers already.

Her hand grasped empty air.

She squatted, legs quivering and still tired from yesterday to peer under the platform.

It was empty.

Her backpack was gone. All her extra clothes, all her food and supplies, were gone.

Chapter Eight

"I don't understand," Dell said. He'd pulled Adeline away from the group to a small outcropping of trees. "You lost your bag?" His voice was an urgent whisper.

"I didn't lose it. I put it under the bottom bunk last night. It was there. And now," she waved a hand impatiently, "it's gone."

"Well, this is new. I've never had a backpack get up and walk away during the night." Dell sighed through his nose, loudly. He knew that it wasn't her fault. But they were deep into the woods now and she had no food, more importantly, no water. Clothes, other supplies … not to mention how it looked to the clients. They were the leaders after all.

"I don't know what to tell you," she said. "I didn't do this on purpose. All I know is that I stowed the bag last night and this morning it's gone."

He pinched the bridge of his nose under his glasses, trying to rein in the stress he was feeling.

"And you didn't hear anyone come into the cabin? Or leave it in the middle of the night?"

Adeline shook her head.

"I apologize," he said, dropping his hand and looking at her. Her eyes were guarded and there was an emotion there that he didn't recognize, which in turn made him uncomfortable. It was his job to know what people were feeling, even when they didn't know themselves. He was good at it and the fact that he couldn't read her right now made a tight band in his gut.

"Let's talk to the others. We'll pool resources, ask if the other women have some extra clothes to loan you." He'd purposefully lowered his voice a register and now it sounded more calming and not so irritated. The heat still pressed hot in his chest, though. To show ineptitude to the group, to ask for their help … he didn't like it.

But what else could be done?

They were an hour late breaking up camp. It was going to be tight getting to Shiny Creek and the lean-to as it was. He hadn't anticipated the early morning delays. He glanced back and saw the group trudging behind him.

Dust it off. Get going. There wasn't any changing what had happened. He couldn't imagine where the pack had ended up, but there wasn't any point in lamenting its fate further. "It is what it is." The popular saying popped into his head. Even though it was trite in this case it was also true.

He'd loaned Adeline an extra windbreaker and some socks, though they'd have to be camp socks. They were two sizes too big and wouldn't fit inside her hiking boots. Maria had given her pants and another pair of socks and Alaska had begrudgingly offered an extra shirt. Gabe had given Adeline an extra flannel button down and they had each divvied up the food and water. Shiny Creek would have plenty more water. They had their charcoal filtering water bottles so a safe supply was nearly guaranteed.

The shoulder straps of his pack dug into his shoulders but instead of causing irritation, he welcomed the discomfort. Life got too soft too easily. It was only here, in the woods, that he felt most like himself. Unless one is uncomfortable, his grandfather used to tell him, he isn't really alive.

That's why, when the question, *should they turn back*, bounced unwelcome into his head, Dell shook it free immediately. They weren't quitting. Things would go according to plan the rest of the weekend. He'd make sure of it.

A noise split the quiet of their rustling steps through the undergrowth, a deep, familiar rumble.

"Thunder," someone behind him said.

Dell picked up his pace, silently cursing the weather reporter and his inaccurate prediction about sunny skies and warmer-than-usual temps. There were miles to cover before they'd stop for a rest. It was best to put the most distance possible between the group and the temptation of the parking lot.

The pack was gone. Long gone. Tossed over the side of the mountain it had wobbled its way down into a ravine, end over end. Summersaulting until, finally, it settled among piles of dusty, dry leaves and tangled berry brambles.

She would leave now, surely.

Wouldn't she?

Alaska pulled her thoughts back to the present and returned to counting her footsteps—*three-hundred and forty-one, three-hundred and forty-two*—and tried to stop thinking about David. Or rather, about David and Dr. Preston. If she *was* really a doctor. And Alaska wouldn't bet on that. It was probably just David's attempt to level the playing field, make them appear as equals.

She snorted, then caught herself. She'd missed the last three steps—*three hundred and forty-six, three hundred and forty-seven*—and anyway, what did it matter? David had to realize by now that he'd asked a bumbling idiot to lead the trip with him. What kind of moron loses her own backpack when it's all that she has to keep track of in the entire world?

Three hundred and eighty-one, three hundred and eighty-two. Alaska could hear the other group members huffing and puffing far behind. The sound made her want to laugh out loud. Actually, what she really wanted to do was yell over her shoulder, "ever heard of a gym?" but of course, she didn't.

David was stopped up ahead, looking down at something. She jogged the last stretch of path to catch up with him.

"What is it?" she asked, barely breathing hard. If this was considered an average to difficult section of the trail, she was golden.

"Hmm?" David asked, distracted. He was studying a paper with thin, tendril-like lines on it. Alaska pressed closer than she needed to. She could feel the heat of his arm against hers.

"I'm just rechecking coordinates and the guidebook. It says there's a large cave up there." He looked up, pointed to the right, up a steep stretch of wooded ground. "Might be a good place to take a rest before the rain comes in."

As though the clouds overhead could hear him, thunder rolled across the sky, louder than before. Lightning followed seconds later.

"It's getting close," she said, noting the lapse of time between the two. "We can go check it out, before the others catch up." She looked at him, expecting a nod. Instead, he was frowning.

"I don't think we'd better go on alone. They might miss us and continue going on the trail."

"I doubt they'll be here for another half-hour," Alaska wanted to say. But didn't. Instead she said, "Right. Maybe I could go and check it out while you wait here."

"Oh, I don't think that's a good—"

"It will save us some time, Da … Dr. O'Dell. We don't really have a lot of that to waste right now, do we? Look," she said, lowering her voice. "The other women aren't keeping up so well. They're not in great shape, plus I think they're discouraged," she shrugged. "We barely have enough dry clothes between us now." She emphasized "now" slightly. "If they get soaked on top of everything else—"

David was nodding.

"You're right. But maybe I should go look for the cave while you wait here. I've hiked these woods before."

"And you know where it is?"

David shook his head, frowned. "Well, no."

"I'm great at orienteering," Alaska said. "Let me have the book and the compass and I'll be back in five minutes. Ten at the most. If I get misplaced, I'll use this," she smiled, waggling the bright red whistle hanging on a cord around her neck. He'd given each of them one at the start of the hike along with instructions to blow three times in succession if they were to get lost.

Honestly, Alaska had nearly tossed the thing alongside the trail. What was she, a five-year-old? Instead, she'd dutifully put it around her neck. The other use—in case they ran into a bear—seemed like a good reason to keep it handy.

"All right," David was saying, handing her the open book and the compass. "And you're certain you feel comfortable finding your way?"

"Absolutely," she said.

She turned and started walking through the undergrowth in the direction David had pointed earlier. She waited until she was far enough from the trail that he couldn't see her through the foliage. Then she closed the book and pocketed the compass. She had no idea how to use either. But that certainly wouldn't have impressed David.

Besides, she was looking for a cave which required big, tall rocks. How hard could it be to find?

Chapter Nine

"It's been more than an hour," Gabe said to Addie. "What do you think happened?"

Addie was staring into the woods beside the trail. Was she hoping that if she looked hard enough she could make the rest of the group reappear?

Alaska was gone.

Lost. Misplaced. Disoriented. Injured? Addie shivered. God, she hoped not.

She put a comforting hand on Gabe's shoulder. "It's going to be fine. I'm sure she just got a little misplaced. We'll find her or she'll find us."

They had waited at first, when the group had caught up to Dell. Then they'd waited a little more. Finally, Dell had gone into the woods alone, looking for Alaska. When he returned a half hour later, the group had split into two groups. One stayed on the trail waiting in case Alaska reappeared and also guarding the rest of the supplies. The other had gone into the woods, looking for Alaska, calling her name and checking for signs of the missing hiker. But so far … nothing.

The air was damp and the temperature had dropped in the past twenty minutes or so. Addie shivered, clenching her arms around her middle to trap in any heat possible.

"The cave is only five or ten minutes from here," Dell had said earlier. "She said she was an expert with orienteering. I just assumed …" his voice had trailed away, so Addie had filled in the gap.

"I'm sure she's fine. Maybe she stopped for a rest and fell asleep." Even in her own ears it was a lame explanation.

"Yeah, right." Clark spoke up. "What's she got, that disease where you fall asleep wherever and whenever?"

Dell had run a hand over his face, then squeezed the skin between his eyes together. Addie recognized it as a frustrated gesture.

"Narcolepsy," he said. "And no, not that I know of. Look. She can't have gotten far," he said. "But we need to find her, find her trail before the rain comes in and washes away any signs of where she's been." The thunder had moved past them to the east, and thankfully, so far, no more rain had fallen.

"What do you expect to find in this," Clark asked now, waving to the thick undergrowth beside the trail. "It's not like there are going to be neat footprints to follow."

Dell had sighed. "No. But there will be other signs. Broken branches, flattened foliage. Let's split the group up and start looking."

He hadn't said, but they'd all understood. Besides the primary goal of finding Alaska was the secondary issue: she had the only guidebook.

Dell took Clark and Maria, leaving Addie with Gabe alongside the trail.

Gabe looked at her now, arms crossed over his chest. He didn't look cold though, just pensive.

"How are you holding up?" Addie asked. He and Alaska were friends, or friendly at least. He must be even more worried than she was.

"Fine," he said then turned from looking into the woods to look at her instead. His eyes were a strange color. She hadn't noticed it before. Probably hadn't been this close to him. A sort of bluish lavender color. Unfortunately, in his thin, pale face they made him look odder.

"How did you get into this anyway?" he was asking. Addie glanced down, rubbed her hands over her arms again.

"Dr. O'Dell knew that I'd been backpacking before and asked if the trip was something I was interested in. Ecotherapy is such an effective method of treatment—"

"No, I didn't mean the trip," he interrupted. "Just, you know. Working as a therapist. How'd you decide that sitting around listening to people's problems was what you wanted to do with your life?"

"Oh. I …" Addie's voice trailed away. "When you put it like that, it does seem like sort of an unusual job to seek out." She chuckled and Gabe smiled. He had a good smile. It made up for the strange eyes and too-big nose.

"You'll appreciate this," she said. "I was actually interested in art, early on."

"Hah! I knew it," Gabe said.

"Really?" Addie asked.

"I can usually recognize other artists on an intuitive level," Gabe said. The way he said it made him sound irritatingly smug. "Anyway, go on. How did you get from art to counseling?"

"Well, for a while I thought maybe I would do just that: pursue art counseling. But the way it worked out a traditional counseling degree was more of a straight shot. I'd had my kids in the middle of my college years, so honestly, I just wanted to finish and start working. My ex-husband …" Addie's voice drifted. Too much personal information. Gabe wasn't her client but he was still a client, not a new friend.

"Sorry. I'm getting off track. To answer your question: I like to help people. I'm nauseous around blood and other bodily fluids so medical training was out of the question. But I find the mind and human nature fascinating. It's a good fit," she said.

"I'll bet art was too, though."

She shrugged. "Did you always know you wanted to be an artist?" she asked.

Gabe chuckled. "Yes. There was no question. I was that kid who was so involved with finger painting in preschool that the teacher had to pry my fingers from the tubs of paint to go play outdoors."

Addie laughed. "And yet here you are," she said, waving a hand around the forest. "Stepping outside your comfort zone and spending time in nature."

Gabe smiled, but it quickly turned to a frown. He looked toward the woods again.

"What do you think happened to her? Alaska isn't one to go quietly. If something or someone came after her—"

"I wouldn't worry too much about wild animals," Addie said. "The animal she saw was likely just a bobcat, like Dr. O'Dell said. It was probably more afraid of her than she was of it."

"I wasn't thinking about that. There are probably other hikers. You hear those stories in the news about women being abducted while hiking, carted off to some cabin and killed. Or worse." Addie glanced at Gabe. He was smiling at her but now the smile didn't look quite as nice. She shivered again. And this time it wasn't from the cold.

"I'm sure that's not what happened," she said. But her voice sounded thin, unconvinced. "She just got misplaced. Besides, those situations, where women are abducted while hiking, they happen once every ten years or so. It's not as frequent as the media makes it seem."

Gabe raised his eyebrows. "It's been about that length of time since I've last heard of it happening." He glanced at her. "Maybe it's that time again."

Something in his face, not just his words, made a sickly feeling crawl up Addie's backbone. She tried to shake it off, smiled at him and moved back toward the packs, mumbling something about trying to find another jacket. She could feel his eyes on her.

Following her.

Chapter Ten

Maria trudged behind Dr. O'Dell, staying far enough back that she wasn't stepping on his heels. Barely. Close enough so that she could reach out and grab him if she needed to. Literally.

Why? Why? Why? The words bounced around in her brain. Why had she left her warm, safe and comfortable apartment for this? She'd wanted to challenge herself, not have a nervous breakdown.

A branch snapped to her left and she gasped, whirling in that direction. It was just Clark though, shoving his way through the bushes and low-hanging branches. Dr. O'Dell had asked them to be very careful, to walk directly behind him, so that they wouldn't chance trampling any signs Alaska had left. But Clark wasn't listening.

It had started to rain and fat drops slid off the big man's floppy fisherman's hat and onto the orange poncho he was wearing. He looked like a traffic cone.

"See anything yet?" Dr. O'Dell asked, ignoring the fact that the other man wasn't following his directions. Clark nodded in response.

Maria's heart jumped hard in her chest.

"You found footprints?" she asked, already breathing out a sigh of relief.

He shook his head.

"No. Not the woman. The cave. It's just over there," he pointed a calloused finger in the direction he'd just come from. "Nice and dry. There's an old fire ring we could use to warm up. Maybe she's in there, further back. I didn't go in too far."

Dr. O'Dell frowned and looked back toward the path ahead. Well, not a path exactly. More an overgrown tangle of bushes and pine saplings and mounds and mounds of decaying leaves.

"I'm going to keep looking," he said. He turned to Maria. "You go with Clark and the others to the cave. Get dry and warm up."

"Oh," Maria said. "What if you get misplaced? Or hurt? How will we find you?" Her voice sounded stronger than she felt. She knew she was the weakest link in the group. If this was a reality TV show, she'd already have been voted off. Probably in the parking lot.

Clark grunted. "You coming or not?" His eyes were shadowed and his lips pulled into a mean line.

Maria bit her lip. She looked from one man to the other. Not only did it feel unsafe for Dr. O'Dell to go on alone, but she didn't like the idea of being with Clark. Even for the short amount of time until the others joined them at the cave.

"Go ahead, Maria," Dr. O'Dell's voice was gentle. "I'll be fine. I'm just going to circle around a few more times and then meet you."

Maria nodded. Her throat felt dry and tight. She trudged behind Clark who didn't bother holding onto any branches after he passed through. They sailed back into Maria's face and arms, drenching her further and making it hard to see. She let him get a little ahead, so that the branches stopped slapping backward after him.

And then the opening of the cave was in front of them suddenly. It was weird: the monotony of leaves and branches breaking unexpectedly into a hulking rock formation. Maria looked around.

"We should get the others," she said.

"I'll go let them know. Dr. Preston can carry your pack." Before she could offer to go with him, he waved a hand toward the cave. "Just get in and clear some space for us. We'll be back in a few minutes."

He left before she could say anything. She didn't feel safe with him around, but wasn't relishing the thought of entering the dark cave by herself either. If only she'd grabbed a flashlight from her pack. Even though the light outside wasn't bright, it was even more dim inside the cave. It had a dark, musty smell too, like clothes that've been in the washer too long or towels from the beach, forgotten in a bag.

She felt her jacket pockets out of habit and grinned when her hand felt a familiar cylindrical lump. Her backup flashlight. She switched it on and moved into the mouth of the cave. It was quiet in here, compared to the outdoors where the wind blew and the tree branches moaned and creaked overhead. She heard water, somewhere far in the back. Maybe a stream ran through the cave somewhere? She shivered.

The flashlight beam illuminated a couple of feet in front of her. She swept the light to the right and then the left. Nothing but assorted rocks, a lot of dry leaves, and a few branches. The fire ring Clark had mentioned was several feet from the opening. Probably so that the smoke would drift out but the rain couldn't get in and douse the flames.

Wind rattled the branches nearest the cave's entrance and Maria unconsciously stepped back. Her foot caught on a branch and she twisted her ankle, yelped and dropped her flashlight. Squatting, she rubbed the area. Tears sprang to her eyes. Just what she needed on top of everything else. Why, why, why had she ever agreed to come on this trip? She could be doing what she normally did on Sunday: attend Mass with her mother and sister, listen to them bicker and argue over a lunch that she barely touched, spend the afternoon reading. If she was really adventurous, she would go for a walk in the park near her apartment.

The tears fell faster. Normalcy called like a Siren. Maria continued to rub the ankle with one hand, the other reaching for the light. Deep breaths. Big, deep breaths. The others would be back soon. She groped for the flashlight, unable to see through the tears and the dimness in the cave.

How long till they got here?

Chapter Eleven

They were noisy when they entered the cave, their clothes making a *swish, swish, swish,* sound, voices loud in the dark space. Clark grunted when he saw Maria standing there, shining her light into the rear of the cave. Stupid, clueless woman. He should have sent her back to get the other two. Though she would have probably gotten lost.

"Be nice if we had some of the floor cleared for our stuff," he muttered and started kicking at the dried leaves and the few broken branches that littered the area.

"I'm sorry," Maria said. Her voice was quiet but still bounced off of the stone walls. She moved to start removing some of the debris.

"We'll all feel better," the woman doctor said, "once we get dry and warm. Clark, would you please see if you can find the matches and gather any dry grass or leaves to start the fire?"

He was about to tell her where she could go but didn't. Hell, he was cold and wet. A fire sounded like a good idea.

"Yes, ma'am," he said, saluting her with one finger.

"I'll check further back, see if there are any dry branches." This was the other guy, the wimpy one.

Clark grunted and pulled his pack toward the wall of the cave. He leaned it against the wall there and started pawing through his stuff, looking for matches. They were in a zip-closed baggie in the big inner pocket. His hand felt tightly bundled rolls of extra clothing, a pair of socks, then another, a small pot, some of the crinkly packets of dehydrated food. The pot. He moved his hand back in that direction. The matches had fit perfectly in the little stainless steel pot, along with emergency candles. His fingers felt around in the hollow pot but there was no smooth sided plastic baggie. No matches.

He swore under his breath. They must have come loose when he tossed the pack down on the trail earlier. His gut twisted and face grew hot.

"Did one of you take the matches?" His voice was louder than he intended. Maria gasped and Dr. Preston jumped slightly. The words bounced around the cave, echoing off the damp stone walls.

"No," Dr. Preston said. "We didn't go in your pack."

"Him either?" Clark yanked his head in the direction of where Gabe disappeared.

"I told you no," said the lady shrink. There was a pause. Then, "The matches are gone?" Her voice was gentle.

Clark's gut grew tighter still. His head had the familiar feeling: as though there were a metal band around it and someone was screwing it tighter and tighter. He swore under his breath and turned his pack upside down, shaking it hard.

"Well they sure as hell aren't where I put them."

Two minutes later the entire contents of the nylon pack were strewn around his feet. No matches. And that wasn't the only thing missing. The emergency candles, half of his food, one of two pairs of extra socks and a first aid kit were gone. Red heat coursed up Clark's chest and into his arms. The heat overtook him, the red anger that welled in his chest and without warning, without even meaning to, he swung his fist into the nearest wall. Pain bloomed over his knuckles and radiated up his arm. Little shock waves rode up toward his core. The velocity snapped his teeth together.

"Clark! Clark, stop, please." Dr. Preston rushed to his side, holding her hands out in a pleading motion. Removing a bandana from around her neck, she wrung the rain out. "That's not going to help anything."

"Someone was in my pack," his voice was hoarse. "They took stuff—not just the matches—the candles, most of my food, the first aid kit—"

"Well slamming your first into stone isn't going to help things. Let me see that," she bent over his hand. Blood was coming out of the knuckles. He could feel the warmth running over the cold skin. He looked up, toward the ceiling.

"What the hell is that?" His voice, like his veins, had just turned to ice.

Addie's fingers shook as she bandaged Clark's knuckles. Already the skin was swelling, tightening over bone. Was it fear or hunger or cold making her hands shake? Maybe all three.

If they couldn't start a fire …

Hypothermia wasn't unlikely. They were all soaked to the skin and cold. A gust of wind tore around the opening of the cave, sending another onslaught of spiky rain and sodden leaves in. Clark's voice cut the relative quiet of the cave cleanly. His question asked with such a sense of dread made the flesh of her spine crawl.

Addie looked up, first at him and then, slowly, at the ceiling above them.

A pentagram, or something like it, was painted into the lowest section of ceiling. There were other symbols around it, strange and unfamiliar. The star itself was nearly three feet in diameter.

"What in the world—"

"What is it, some kind of satanic lair?" Clark said, looking from the ceiling to Addie and back again.

"Shh," Addie said. "She'll hear—"

"Hear what?" Maria said. Maria's voice near Addie's shoulder made her jump causing her to bump Clark's hand.

"Ouch."

"Sorry," Addie mumbled.

Maria followed Clark's gaze up to the ceiling.

"Oh my God. What is that?" Maria's hand went automatically to her throat. She stood there a moment, her face losing color. She swayed as though the wind was holding her upright and without it she would collapse.

"It's nothing. Just some silly high school kids' prank," Addie said. She glanced at Clark and mouthed, "help me out."

"Yeah," Clark said, finally tearing his eyes from the drawing. "We used to do stuff like that all the time when I was in school."

"Really?" Maria asked. Her voice sounded far away. She looked far away, lost in a trance, staring at the markings.

"Sure," Clark said. "Young and stupid, right?"

Maria didn't respond. Addie turned toward the younger woman, shook her shoulders gently.

"Maria, I need you to go into your pack and get out the second first aid kit, OK? I need some antibacterial salve for Clark's hand."

"I don't need—" Clark started.

"Yes, you do," Addie said, her voice loud in the small space. She narrowed her eyes at him.

"I'm fine," he said. "I've done worse on a Saturday night at the bar."

"We have to keep it from getting infected," Addie insisted. She smiled at Maria. "Please, get the kit."

Maria nodded, still moving as though in slow motion or a dream.

"She needs a job," Addie said in a whisper to Clark. "Can you please just help me out?"

He grunted.

"Where is Gabe anyway?" she asked, looking into the darkness of the cave. "How many sticks could he find back there?"

"I'll go look for him," Clark said, pulling his hand away. "First let me bandage—"

Another gust of wind tore at the opening of the cave. The

wind screamed around the boundaries of rock. The rain was driving down now, it lashed the trees and fell in hard sheets.

Addie was about to look away, ask Maria if she'd found the kit, when she saw a figure standing at the cave's entrance in the dim light.

Chapter Twelve

Dell was soaked. He was so wet in fact that he was surprised he could even feel the rain anymore. His limbs were trembling, not from the strain of the hike, but from the cold and his sodden clothes.

The first signs of hypothermia: what were they again? His teeth chattered, his glasses, which he'd removed every few feet at first to dry on the damp T-shirt under his raincoat, had fogged over once again. Not that it mattered. Water streamed from the floppy hat and much of the stream cascaded over his face: glasses, nose, chin. He swiped his forearm over his entire face and paused from pushing through the branches in front of him.

Where could she have gone? Ten minutes. Ten minutes it should have taken to get to the cave—and that's if she was walking extremely slowly. Alaska had long legs and a powerful stride, it should have been five.

If she'd been going the right way.

But he'd given her the compass and the map. She'd known how to use them. How could this have happened?

His chattering teeth reminded him that he needed to get warm and dry off. Quickly. He checked his bearings, then looked at the ground for any signs that she'd passed this way: broken branches or footprints in the mud, a snagged thread from her clothes. But there was nothing.

Dell sighed, turned around and was about to start back the way he'd come.

And then he saw it.

A yard or so from where he was standing. A footprint.

Not his, surely. He hadn't been through that section of the woods.

Had he?

Everything was starting to feel the same to him. The trees all the looked the same—wet and dripping. He moved toward the footprint, careful not to smear it. It was large. A deep well where the heel had pressed down the dirt.

Dell blinked. Frowned.

Moved closer.

"This can't be …"

A rumble of thunder drowned out the half-whisper. Dell shivered, hard. There were no markings left by a shoe. No squares or circles or triangles left in the mud, no pattern that the boot or sneaker had left. Instead the heel of the footprint was soft and round and deep. Above it was the outline was smeared but it widened out near the top. It ended with five distinct markings. Where each individual toe had pressed into the mud.

Crack!

A bolt of lightning cut across the darkening sky. Dell

gasped, nearly fell backward. He had to get out of the trees. He pushed blindly back the way he'd come, following the trail he'd left of broken branches and muddy boot prints. The air smelled of smoke. He must be nearing the cave. But then another smell followed, like singed hair.

Jogging blindly, shoving branches and leaves and brambles out of his way, Dell continued on.

"Alaska! Alaska, where are you?" His voice sounded strangled, ineffective.

Thoughts of her huddled in the rain ran through his brain, a movie reel of images of her wet and cold and shivering. But where? Where?

Thunder shook the air around him followed nearly immediately by another crack of lightning. He was blinded momentarily. First from the excruciating light and then from the darkness that followed. Like walking into a dark room after being out in the summer sun, it was impossible to see anything except shapes.

Dell slowed his steps, moving forward cautiously, hands outstretched. Suddenly, his foot hit something heavy and hard. He pitched forward, hands outstretched. He was going down.

He felt warmth and hair.

Maria screamed as the dim figure in the face of the cave started to enter. Clark stood, rooted in place, Addie beside him.

The thunder outside the cave growled loudly and small rocks on the cave floor shook. A slash of lightning split the sky outside the entrance and for a moment illuminated the dark figure.

"Gabe?" Addie rushed forward, pulling the thin man into the cave. "What happened? Are you OK?"

Gabe nodded. His teeth chattered and he spoke between snaps of his jaw. He was soaked. "Followed the cave to the back." *Chatter, chatter.* "It spit me out into the woods." *Chatter, chatter.*

"Why didn't you come back the way you came?" Clark's tone was seared with sarcasm. It said, *are you an idiot?*

Addie frowned at Clark. "It doesn't matter."

She turned to Gabe. "We haven't had luck starting the fire yet but we'll get it going soon. Come and sit down."

She led the shivering man to a large stone nearby and he sat, smiled at her gratefully.

Maria approached, holding a small white box in her hands. Addie thanked her.

"Do either of you have any matches?" she asked. Maria nodded.

"I had two sets and when we reorganized our packs Dr. O'Dell put one in the pile of things to stay behind," Maria looked embarrassed. "But I took it back out when he wasn't looking."

"I'm so glad you did, Maria."

Maria shrugged but her mouth pulled up into a smile.

"Can you get them please?" Addie turned. "Gabe, you'd better change out of those wet things."

He nodded between shivers, then walked to his pack and began to pull things out of it.

Clark grunted and Addie turned to him.

"Let me see your hand, please."

He sighed through his nose, a deep and long sound, but stretched out his hand.

As Addie cleaned the area and smeared on a thin layer of disinfectant, she listened to the rain slashing outside. If Dell wasn't back by the time she was finished, she'd go look for him.

"He should have been back by now," Clark said, as though reading her mind. "Think he's gotten lost?"

"No," she said. But she wasn't so sure. "He's an experienced outdoorsman. I'm sure he could find his way around here with his eyes closed."

"Yeah, well. He didn't do a real good job predicting the weather, did he?"

Addie chewed her lip and added two Band-Aids to the man's hand.

"Sometimes even meteorologists are wrong," she said lightly. "There." Addie surveyed her handiwork. "You're all set."

Clark grumbled something under his breath. Addie put the supplies back into the kit and walked to Maria's pack.

"Let me," Maria said, nearly jumping over a large rock to grab the kit from Addie's hands. "I have it organized in a certain way," she said, apologetically.

Addie smiled. "Any luck with the fire?"

"Yes. I think so."

Gabe was crouched over the fire ring, his clean, dry clothes in a pile beside him. He was blowing through his hands on a small flicker of light. The flame wobbled and bounced and nearly went out.

"Not like that," Clark said. He strode over in two long steps and nearly knocked Gabe over as he bent next to him.

"Hey!"

"You'll put it out," Clark said.

"I think I know how to start a fire. I went to summer camp for years." Gabe steadied himself with a hand to the cave wall closest to him.

Clark snorted in response.

"I'm going out," Addie said. Maria looked at her, eyes wide.

"Why?" she asked.

"To find Dr. O'Dell, see how he is doing with the search. See if he's found anything."

"Like body parts?" Clark asked. A twig with a burning end held between his thick fingers flickered.

"Clark, that's really inappropriate. He may have found signs of where Alaska went. I still think she's fine. She's probably holed up somewhere nearby, in her own cave. Out of the weather," she said, glancing toward the rain.

A distorted noise bent and wobbled through the sheets of rain. A yell? A growl? Addie moved closer to the cave's entrance.

Fingertips of fear danced up her backbone.

There it was again. A strangled cry. Human? Animal?

She turned to the others.

"Did you hear something?"

Chapter Thirteen

When David O'Dell was five years old, he'd fallen into a dry well. Playing with his older brothers—tag was it?—his foot had slipped through some rotted boards. For a second, he'd thought they would hold; there were enough good boards to keep him upright. And then the rest of the flimsy wood had splintered.

That's what he remembered most: the crack of the splintering boards as they broke into a hundred pieces and the feeling as his body passed, weightless, through the blackness below. He didn't remember hitting the ground. Only waking up later to his name being called and a light above which seemed a hundred miles away.

It was the same feeling he had now, falling. Only then he'd been falling feet first into a dry enclosure and this time he was falling headfirst, tripped over an exposed root. The body before him was still warm. The smell of singed flesh and burning hair filled his nostrils. He threw his arms out in front of him instinctively. Felt his forearms connect with flesh and cartilage and bone. He gagged and turned his face away, scrambling to get back up to his feet. The mud on the ground around him sucked and smeared and pulled at his boots and hands.

Finally, he scuttled back far enough to see. Heartbeat drumming in his ears like a percussionist playing an extra-fast fill. His glasses were coated with rain and mud, making it nearly impossible to see. Dell pulled them from his face, wiped them on the hem of his soaking undershirt. He replaced the glasses and let his backpack slide from his shoulders. Laying it gently on the ground he moved forward. The smell made him gag again.

Before him lay a body.

But not Alaska. Not even a human. It was a doe, a large one. She was stretched out across the path, legs extended as though ready to leap over a fence or high patch of brambles. Her hooves were dainty, legs muddy. Shiny eyes stared up at nothing. A jagged path of burned hair stood out dark against her caramel-colored coat where the bolt of lightning had left its mark like Zorro. Smoke and steam rose from the deer's coat. The rain was slackening, just slightly. The light was dim. Growing darker.

Dell stood and looked around him. God, he was cold. His skin felt like rubber, wet and thick. He walked around the doe, left a wide circle. Twenty feet away. Why was the walking so much easier? Downhill, maybe. He shivered. His feet and legs were covered in something heavy. Mud. They were covered in mud. Dell shook his head like a dog shaking off water. Had to get his bearings. Where was he going again? Rain dripped down the collar of his coat. The trickles felt icy against his spine. Strange since his back was already so wet. Back. Backpack. Where was that?

"I'm not sure," Dell said aloud. The sound startled him. He glanced around the woods. Had he said the words? Or someone else? Was someone watching him? Interesting. And strange because his thin felt so sick. Thin felt sick? Dell chuckled under his breath. His legs were shaking.

"I should rest." This time the words came from his mouth, he was sure. Almost sure. He glanced around again. The trees and branches and leaves and pine boughs all looked the same. Where was he? He smelled something.

Smoke. Had he circled back to the deer?

He looked right and left, moving aside the undergrowth in sweeping motions with his arms.

No doe.

Doe a deer. A female deer.

How did the rest of that song go? *Saw a note to follow tea...*

Maybe he would rest. Just for a minute. This pine tree was big and bushy. Dell wished that he could climb in among the branches and sleep, suspended over the wet, muddy earth. Instead he leaned against the trunk.

No. He shook his head.

He should keep moving. He needed to get ... somewhere.

Sitting meant that he could freeze. Hypoberm ... hypodermi ... whatever that was called. Dangerous.

So sleepy, though. Just for a minute.

Dell closed his eyes.

"I didn't hear anything," Clark said. Addie remained by the opening of the cave. She pulled the hood of her rainproof, wind-proof jacket over her head.

It had been a shout or yell of alarm. Hadn't it?

The wind howled around the outside of the cave, bending tree branches.

"It was just the wind," Clark called.

"I'm going to check." The words were brave but her knees were practically knocking together. An image of Ichabod Crane in the Headless Horseman cartoon popped into her mind. Knees knocking, teeth chattering. Addie shook her head, trying to clear the clutter. Maria called something out but Addie had already plunged into the driving rain. The wind ripped the words away and filled her ears with their moans. She held her hands out in front of her.

"Dell? Dr. O'Dell?" she yelled. There was a tickle at the back of her throat and her mouth felt dry. Surprising that anything left could be dry. She called his name again and again, making circles around the cave: first tight and then a spreading out a little further. But never losing sight of it.

Once, when the boys were pre-teens, they'd gone on an overnighter. Michael had wandered off the path, or as he told her later, he'd explored his way away from it. She and Ben had looked for him for what seemed like hours but was probably thirty minutes. Addie remembered the panic climbing up her chest, her breathing becoming choked. She'd held it together, for Ben, but left on her own she wasn't so sure she'd have been able to.

They'd used the same technique she was now, making

wider and wider circles, but always keeping the camp in sight. Addie was comfortable in the woods but not off the trail. That was always a mistake.

A root snagged the toe of her boot and Addie stumbled, caught herself on a pine branch. The scent of Christmas filled her nose and she breathed deeply. What was that?

Addie peered at a lumpy brown clod of mud. The rain was lessening now but the light was dim, overhead gray clouds continued to drown out the sun. She moved closer, bent down.

Not mud. At least, not only mud.

A boot.

Chapter Fourteen

Maria paced around the fire, the fingers in her pocket rubbing a smooth stone. She'd found it earlier near a small brook they'd crossed. It was cool and silky and felt good on her fingertips. The scent of wood smoke was heavy in the air, the damp wood producing more every minute. Maria breathed deeply and nearly choked.

"Would you sit down?" Clark said, glancing up at her. He squatted in front of the fire, the flames dancing across his sharp features, making the lines in his face more pronounced.

"Just relax," he said, tossing another small stick onto the fire.

Relax? How was she supposed to do that? The one person familiar to her on this catastrophe of a trip was gone. What if she never came back? Maria glanced at the men, her gaze sliding quickly away as Gabe made eye contact.

She walked toward the opening of the cave, far enough to peer out but not so far that she would get soaked. She turned to the side, glanced back casually. Gabe was still looking at her. His eyes were strange; the firelight made the planes of his face dance and jerk. She swallowed hard, drew her shoulders down. Trying to make herself look more confident than she felt.

"Do you think we should go out and try to find her?" she asked. Her voice sounded thin and reedy competing with the rain slashing.

Clark snorted. "The doctor? She's long gone. O'Dell too, if you ask me. We should start thinking about how we're going to get out of here."

Maria wanted to protest. Instead she just stared.

"She'll be back soon. And will probably bring Dr. O'Dell back with her," Gabe said. He hesitated, then glanced from Maria to the fire and lastly to Clark. "She has a wisdom about her. She'll be the one to get us out of here, watch and see."

"I'll be the one to do that," Clark said, slapping his hands against his thighs. "We've seen how you navigate something as simple as a pile of rocks," he waved a big hand around the cave. "And she's not going to be leading us anywhere," he yanked his head in Maria's direction.

Gabe said something that Maria was too far away to hear.

"What's that, prissy?" Clark said, lowering his head like a bull ready to charge.

"I said she'll be back. Dr. Preston." Gabe's voice was louder, stronger.

"I think we should try to get some rest," Maria said, her voice barely more than a squeak. Her palms felt sweaty and her vision wobbled for a few seconds. *Breathe, Maria. Breathe.*

"Sounds good to me," Clark said, pawing through his pack. Maria thought of her tidy apartment and the soft bed that she'd made so neatly yesterday morning. Yesterday? It felt like years ago.

"If Dr. Preston isn't back in fifteen minutes, one of us should go out and look for her," Maria said. Clark didn't say anything but continued rummaging in his pack.

"Who's going to go?" Gabe asked. "I can, if you want."

Maria nodded, smiled. Maybe she'd misjudged him.

"Thank you. Let's wait though, just in case …"

Tears suddenly wet her eyes. Her mantra. *Just in case. Just in case. Just in case.*

She turned her back to the men, and watched the rain bouncing off the large boulders near the opening of the cave. It was lessening, wasn't it? Maria fingered the stone in her pocket and concentrated on her breathing. Slow breath in. Slow breath out. Slow breath in …

Addie crouched and crab-walked toward the feet underneath the tall pine tree. Toes of boots poked up out of the muck, impossible to tell what color. She followed the feet up to legs encased in black rain pants then moved closer to the legs. Craning her neck, she could just see underneath the low-hanging boughs of the tree.

"Dell!" her voice was a yell but didn't bring a reaction of any kind. The doctor's face was pale, his glasses grimy and his face and hands smeared with mud. Addie crawled forward, put a hand on his face just over his nose. Her hands trembled and shook. If he was breathing, she couldn't feel it.

She moved her hands down to his chest. Waited.

There. A breath, followed by another.

How was she going to get him out of here?

"Dell? Dell." She shook his shoulders firmly. No response. She shook harder but he didn't move, was unconscious. Had he been hit by something? She tried to roll him to the side, check the back of his head. Instead he lolled all the way to the ground, flopped there like a dead fish.

"Dell? Can you hear me?" Addie reached over and slapped his cheek. Her frozen fingers barely registered the blow but Dell's eyelids fluttered. She did it again. And again. Finally, the third time, his eyes opened fully. Addie removed his glasses, helped him up into a seated position. She rubbed the spectacles on her T-shirt—the one piece of clothes that was relatively dry—and replaced them on his face.

"Wha ... happen ...?"

"I'm not sure. But you're OK now. We just have to figure out a way to get you back to camp."

"Camp."

"Well, the cave. It's our temporary camp." She wanted to ask if he'd had any success finding Alaska but assumed since he was alone, the answer was no.

"Can you get up if I help?" Addie slid one of the doctor's arms over her shoulders and tried to rise to her feet. Her legs trembled. Then she stumbled and fell.

"Sorry," she said. "Can you move your body at all?"

Dell shook his head, then nodded.

"I don't know," he sounded mystified.

"Well, can you try?" Addie asked.

"OK," he said. She felt a light pressure from the arm slung around her shoulders. On the second try they both made it halfway to a standing position before falling.

Addie cursed under her breath.

"I sorry," Dell said, his voice slurred. "I feel … strange."

"It's not your fault," Addie replied. "Let's give it a minute and we'll try again." Her eyes checked the area around and under the tree. "Where's your pack?"

"My pack? Hmmm," his voice wandered away for a minute. "Not sure. Deer … got."

"Deer guts?"

Dell's eyes were closing again.

"No, no, don't fall asleep." She braced her back against the tree, then crouched, using it to support her. "Give me your arm. Let's try again. We've got to get you back to camp; there's a fire going and you can get warmed up," her voice had changed slightly, from that of grateful peer to that of a mother coaxing her child to do something he didn't want to.

This time their legs worked in conjunction. Addie didn't stop but staggered back the way she'd come. "I'll come back and try to find your pack once we get you settled and dry," she said. Cold rain bit into her neck and her hand gripping Dell's started to slip. She readjusted, clamped on to his hand harder and continued walking.

The trek back to the cave seemed to take hours but Addie was sure it was less than ten minutes. Her thighs burned with the effort of supporting a grown man's weight, her arm, twisted in a weird way to not lose her grip on Dell's torso, ached. She was breathing heavily when the entrance of the cave came into view. She paused, just for a moment to catch her breath. Mistake. Dell wobbled to the side and started to slide to the ground. His eyes were closed.

"Hey!" Addie yelled. "Can someone help me?"

There was no response from the cave entrance.

Gabe stared into the flames. Clark had found some drier branches further back in the cave—branches that he, Gabe—had apparently been too unobservant to notice. A snap cut the air, sparks from the fire rushed upward. He shivered, held his hands out to the flames. He glanced to the rear of the cave. What had he seen? Eyes. Staring as he approached. Or was it the light of his flashlight reflecting off of something? Something that glinted and glowed. His stomach rumbled and then pinched. How many hours since he's last eaten?

He drew his pack closer, glanced around. Clark had laid down in a crevice between some rocks, using his pack for a pillow. Maria stood beyond him, near the entrance to the cave. One hand in her pocket the other gripping the cave wall. She was beautiful, even after two days without a shower or comb.

Gabe shook his head, trying to clear it. Why had he wanted to get his pack out? He opened the zipper slowly, pulled back the flap. Perhaps if he saw it, he'd remember. His hands poked and prodded, drawing out extra clothes, a metal pot.

Then his hand closed around the nylon bag. Dr. O'Dell's

gun. Maybe he should use it on the asshole that thought he was so smart. Clark would have a different look on his face if Gabe waved this in his face. Gabe's heartbeat sped up slightly, his breath came a little faster.

"Hungry?" a voice asked.

Gabe jumped, the nylon bag fell to the ground with a dull thud. He grabbed it, stuffed the thing back into his pack. Maria stood nearby. He hadn't even heard her approaching.

"Yeah, I guess," he cleared his throat. "I was just looking for a bar or something easy to eat. How much water do you have left?" His voice sounded surprisingly normal, steady.

She shrugged. Standing a few feet away, the firelight barely illuminated her face.

"Enough, I think," she said. "Do you need some?"

"No," Gabe responded. "Not yet anyway."

"I'm going to put mine out near the opening, to catch some of the rainwater," Maria said. "Can I fill yours too?"

"Sure," he said. He found it among the other items and handed it to her. Her fingers were warm when his brushed against them but she jerked back as though his were flames. The rain was slacking a bit, coming down in thin sheets now rather than heavy walls.

He looked past Maria, saw motion near the entrance. What was that? Gabe stood halfway. The smell of the smoky interior suddenly made his empty stomach roil.

There it was again. Something moving toward the entrance. Something hulking and bulky. Gabe pointed to the mouth of the cave and Maria gasped.

Chapter Fifteen

"Addie!" Maria's cry bounced around the stone walls. She rushed to the entrance, nearly tripping on a large stone. Clark, watching from his sleeping bag, bolted upright. He'd been dreaming … something about a giant cloudless stretch of sky; a sense of falling.

"Help me, please," the woman doctor's voice said. Clark rubbed his hands over his eyes which felt gritty, and stood up. The sleeping bag fell away and the air outside of it was cold. He grunted, stuffed his feet back into the damp boots nearby and walked to the cave's entrance. Prissy boy wasn't going to be a big help. He was still sitting at the fire, mouth partly open, staring at the entrance.

"Where've you been?" he said when he drew closer. The smell of smoke from the fire mixed in the air with another scent he couldn't place. Preston was supporting the weight of O'Dell, who looked half-dead. His eyelids fluttered open and then closed behind his glasses, his body as limp as a pile of noodles.

"Give him here," Clark said. He squatted a little, slid the

man's wet arm around his neck and pulled him close to the fire. The fire that was starting to go out. Couldn't anyone in this group do anything without being given instruction?

"Hey," he said, his voice booming in the closed space. "You wanna throw some new branches on that thing?" Gabe's head snapped toward him as though he'd knocked him across the head.

"Wh … what?" he said. "There aren't any more," the thin man said. His voice was whiny and it grated on Clark's stretched nerves. Clark snorted, half-dragged and half-dropped O'Dell on his side near the fire.

"Careful!" one of the women said. "Don't hurt him."

"He'll be fine," Clark said. Then he turned, pointed to the younger woman. "Go out back and get some more branches. I made a small pile of the extras. To the left."

The woman looked at him, eyes wide.

"I'll go," the doctor said. She was shivering, soaked through. "It's probably better if I keep moving to stay warm."

"No," Maria said. "You should find some dry clothes. Look in my pack." She pointed to the big nylon sack near the cave wall. "I'll get the wood."

"I'll come with you. Just wait for me to grab some clothes," Dr. Preston said. Together the women bent over the pack, and after retrieving a few items, went to the rear of the cave.

"He needs to get stripped out of the wet stuff," Dr. Preston called. "Put him in his sleeping bag and get him as close to the fire as possible."

As if I need to be told. Clark stomped around the fire, making room for the doctor's sleeping bag. What a dumbass. Dr. O'Dell brought them out here and he's the one who ends up with hypothermia. Some expert.

"I wonder if there was any sign of Alaska," Gabe asked the empty air.

"Get his sleeping bag laid out, would you?" Clark said, squatting near O'Dell. His thighs ached and there was a spot on the right of his spine that pinched. He undressed O'Dell roughly and together he and the artist stuffed him into the sleeping bag. Clark was breathing heavily by the time they were done and glad to sit on the edge of his own sleeping bag.

"I'll get a Mylar blanket to put in there with him," Dr. Preston said, her voice bouncing around the stones and rocks. She was dressed in pants that were too short, an ill-fitting, but dry shirt, and a polar fleece jacket pulled on but unzipped. Her arms were full of branches in various sizes.

"How is he doing?" Dr. Preston asked. Clark shrugged but nodded. "He'll be fine. Probably. Got any soup in your pack? Oh," he said, remembering, "I guess not. You got any?" He turned to look at Gabe.

"Sure, I think."

The man sat, unmoving.

"Get it out." Clark could feel the heat climbing up from his torso into his face. Stupid, worthless …

"OK." The thin man said and moved toward his pack nearby. Maria emerged from the back, more sticks and branches in her arms.

"I found this too," she said, dropping the load and adding a small pile of dry grass tangled with leaves from her pockets. "I thought it might help with the fire, to make the damp wood catch."

"Thank you, Maria," Dr. Preston said.

Not bad. Smarter than Da Vinci, that's for sure.

"I found a Mylar blanket. It's yours, Maria. Do you mind if we use it for Dr. O'Dell?"

"No, go ahead," Maria said. Her fingers were already sorting the pile of branches into small, medium and larger groups. "I'll work on the fire. Unless you'd rather," she glanced at Clark who shook his head.

"Have at it," he said. He stood again and stretched, then retrieved a collapsible bottle from his pack and walked to the front of the cave. Might as well make good use of the rain.

There was a change in the air that was almost palpable. It felt—Clark couldn't describe it exactly—but something. A sort of comradery or organization to the group that hadn't been there before. He snorted softly, shook his head. Now who was getting soft? None of them would be in this situation if it hadn't been for O'Dell and that stupid woman playing Tarzan. Who gets so completely lost by walking five minutes from a marked hiking trail? An ass, that's who. And what kind of outdoorsman gets the weather wrong? Not just a little wrong either, like a sprinkle instead of a perfectly dry day. No, the kind where you end up with a monsoon in place of sunshine and baby blue skies.

How long had he been working with O'Dell? Six months? Eight at the most. And what had he really gotten out of the sessions? Nothing, other than the note that allowed him to go back to work. It hadn't brought Sabrina back. Not that he even wanted her back. But he wanted something, didn't he? Something different than working twelve-hour days and drinking in front of the TV and spending the weekends with different women, telling himself that it was good. But still feeling that hollow spot inside when he was alone again.

The rain was slackening. Clark twisted the cover off the jug and positioned it under a stream of water coming from a rock near the cave's entrance. He would filter it later, if they needed to use it. When he went back in, he'd tell the others that an inventory would need to be done. They needed to take stock of what everyone had and distribute the food and water to each pack that was left.

He heard a groan from the interior of the cave and glanced over his shoulder. A mist coming from the rain on the rocks nearby had covered his face. The water itched and he rubbed his face. O'Dell was moaning in his sleeping bag.

Clark retraced his steps. The fire was already burning brightly, licking at the dry leaves and clumps of parched grass.

"Not bad," he said gruffly to the woman kneeling in front of the ring. She smiled and glanced at him, then went back to feeding small branches to the flames.

The woman counselor and Gabe were staring at him, he could tell without looking. He ignored them and walked to his pack.

"I'm getting some fresh water in case we need it," he said,

jerking his head toward the entrance of the cave. "We need to take an inventory of the supplies we have left, redistribute stuff around."

"That's a good idea," Dr. Preston said. O'Dell moaned again.

"You put that blanket on him already?" he asked.

She nodded.

"You'd better give him some water. Juice, if you've got it. Something sugary is your best bet. He's alert enough he won't choke," Clark said.

Dr. Preston looked at the doctor lying in front of her. His eyes were open and he was looking around as far as he could without moving his head.

"You're awake," she said, moving closer. "Can you take a few sips of liquid?"

O'Dell nodded.

"Here," the artist said. He'd been rummaging around in his pack. "I brought this for a treat tonight but you can use it." He handed Dr. Preston a packet of hot cocoa.

"Let's get a pot over the fire with a little water in it," she said.

"Give him some regular water in the meantime," Clark said, moving to his own pack and bringing out a half-full plastic bottle. "He needs liquids."

Dr. Preston smiled at him.

"Thanks," she said, taking the bottle.

Clark frowned and sat back on his sleeping bag. His legs felt itchy and restless so he stood up again.

"I'm going out back, look for some more wood for the

fire. We need enough to last the night at least." As if in response the rain outside the cave lashed out, wetting the first couple of feet of the stone structure's entrance.

"Thank you," Dr. Preston said again. Clark pretended not to hear.

Chapter Sixteen

"Is he gone?" Gabe asked.

He was so close to Addie that she jumped, nearly spilling the water bottle in the process.

"Clark? Yes, I think so. Why?"

Gabe motioned to her to come closer. He was kneeling on a folded shirt near his backpack.

"I want to show you something. You too," he glanced at Maria and she nodded, walked over. She kept her distance though, standing a few paces behind Addie and Gabe.

"I found this when I was in the back of the cave. It's old, really old."

He held out his hand, turning it over so that the palm was right-side up. On it, sat a small, rusted box. At first Addie thought it was one of those that you buy filled with breath mints. But when she looked more closely, she could see that it was bigger. There was no label left, the moist interior of the cave had obliterated it and rusted the box completely.

"It's got something inside that I think you might both

like to see," Gabe said and handed it to Addie.

She took the box in her own hand. It was lighter than she expected. The little hinges creaked and then gave a little "pop," before opening. She turned her body, until the light from the fire washed over it.

There was some sort of hard fabric inside. Addie glanced up at Gabe.

"Open it. That's just some kind of protective layer."

She pulled the packet free, and set the box gently on a stone beside her, then unfolded the thick, heavy outer wrap. Inside, were several smaller pieces of brittle paper. Newspaper clippings.

"How old are these, I wonder?" she asked, but neither Maria or Gabe replied.

She pulled them gently from the protective layer and laid each one on her pant leg.

Maria moved in closer, bringing the flashlight with her and shining it on the papers.

"Thank you," Addie said.

"What do they say?" Maria asked.

Addie started to read aloud. The first in the pile was dated 1897, but the month and day were missing. It was short, about two paragraphs of neatly-typed font.

Man Missing on Shiny Creek Trail

Mister James Smithfield, 18 years of age, was reported missing on Tuesday, the seventh of July, 1897. Mister Smithfield was last seen by a group of friends on the Shiny Creek trail in Little River. The group left for a two-day hike, which was purported to convene at Shiny Creek on Wednesday, the eighth of July. However, Mister Smith was last seen entering the woods near the camp that the group had created. He was not seen after this time.

A fellow member of the hiking group and friend, Mister James Winters, stated that he had, "seen a monster," in the woods near the trail where Mister Smithfield was last seen. The area was searched by state officials and there were no signs of foul play. Anyone with details or information to share with authorities is encouraged to contact the local police department.

The next clipping was longer, and with it was a shadowy image taking up most of the left-hand side of the page. Addie squinted and turned the paper in the light, but could only make out a large, dark smudge that looked like a photo of a blurry man. She skimmed the clipping, this one dated ten years later, in October of 1907.

Beast Seen on Trail in Little River

Three hunters found a creature they were not bargaining for when they entered the woods on the fifteenth of October. While the men were hunting grouse and deer, one man, a Mister Daniel Elkhorn, took a photograph of this suspicious looking animal. "It was a man beast," said Elkhorn, who was undeniably shaken after the event. "I have never seen anything like it." The two men he was hunting with, a Mister Sawerst and Mister Cleaver, both from the upper New Hampshire area, claimed to have also seen this beast.

"It rose up on hind legs, walked like a man," said Mister Cleaver. "It had a big shaggy head and moved through the woods real quiet."

The men were uninjured and submitted this photo (at left), as evidence of the creature in the woods which they encountered. Made more sensational, is the fact that this is the same area where a local man, Mister James Smithfield, disappeared more than ten years ago. Prior disappearances in this area have been noted as well in previous years.

"My God," Maria breathed out, her breath warm on Addie's cheek. She had a small crucifix around her neck and her fingers were locked around it, rubbing it unconsciously as she stared at the yellowed paper in Addie's hand.

"What do the others say?"

Addie set the two newspaper clippings to the side and

pulled free another piece of paper. This one was handwritten, in a beautiful, curling script on yellowed notebook paper. Her eyes skimmed the looping words. It looked like a journal entry of some type.

In the event of my demise, I, Jane Rogers, being of sound mind and body do write these words as honest truth. Before my God and my family and friends, I do swear to the validity of what I am about to record here.

I entered these woods on the path also known as Shiny Creek trail, two days ago, on the seventh of September, 1917. I accompanied my husband, Paul, a photojournalist and our friends Deidre and Allan, also photojournalists, to seek answers to the riddle of the disappearance of both James Smithfield in 1897 and three others who went missing in this area of the Green Mountains in years prior. I have included clippings of the two most recent events along the Shiny Creek trail.

These two days have been the strangest of my short life. I cannot record everything that I have seen and heard here in this place and if I did, none would believe me. I will tell only this: that there is a presence here that is full of darkness and evil. It comes crawling from the pit of Hell through the entrance of this cave and into the hearts of the men and women who stay here. Allan is dead. I cannot begin to understand the horror that Deidre would have felt to see her beloved husband kill himself by means of hanging in this very cave where I sit. But she was at least spared this as she went missing several hours before Allan's death. Paul and I have searched and been unable to find her.

Paul is not well. He broke his leg in his attempts to remove Allan's body from where it hung, while I, stupidly I will now reflect, cried helplessly and then was sick outside of the cave. Paul is unwell now. Not just the broken leg but in his mind. He is shouting strange words and fights me when I try to help him outside. I think there must be a fever in his brain. I have done my best to cover Allan's body with stone, but my arms are near useless now and I have no more strength to lift another.

How will I get Paul from this place? And where is Deidre? I long so selfishly for the comforts of home: a warm fire, a hot bath and food to eat. But those things may never again be mine. How can I think of such things when our dear friend is dead and another missing? I should go out again and search for Deidre but …"

The words trail off there, at the end of the page. Addie flipped to the next sheet but there is only a single phrase repeated over and over again. It began in the same beautiful script but then degenerated into a harsh scrawl so sharp and ugly that it's hard to believe it was written by the same hand. The word, over and over fell down the page and ran into the next. "Kill," it said, over and over and over.

Maria started crying, soft sobs wracking her body and Addie put out a hand to steady the young woman. Maria moved away though, back toward the fire where she sat, shakily, and then drew her knees up to her chest. She rocked back and forth, staring into the flames.

"Is it real?" Gabe asked Addie. Then, "Can I see it please?"

Addie handed the papers to him wordlessly and looked back into the little packet of thick paper and the box itself. There was nothing else.

Chapter Seventeen

The rear of the cave was damp, more so than the front. The sounds of the fire and low murmur of voices were quickly replaced by the echoes of his footsteps and a steady torrent of water falling from somewhere above. Clark flashed his light around. There were no open areas in the ceiling. The beam bounced off of rocks and jutting stone, making eerie shadows on the walls.

When he was a kid, him and his brother used to stay in the caves behind their house. Those were the good old days, when kids still went outside without their parents pinning them with tracking devices or giving them tablets and computers to stare at for hours and then wondering why little Johnny or Joann turned into a lard ass. He snorted.

Him and Bobby had kept a couple of flashlights in a broken plastic bin in the cave's entrance. They used to go out there when their parents would fight. That meant that they'd spent a lot of time exploring the dark hollows. He wasn't sure which had been better—the exploring—knowing that danger was all around—or looking at the hundreds of tiny, furry bodies hanging from the cave's ceilings.

Clark bounced the light up high in the cave now. There—bats hung in tiny groups near the corners of the high ceiling. They didn't move when the light beam hit them. Probably already hibernating. He moved to the left of a jutting stone tower in front of him, his light beam picking out piles of branches. Along the side of the wall there were more of the grasses that Maria had collected. Had an animal dragged them in, thinking it was going to make a bed for hibernation? Moving to the brush, he set his flashlight on a large stone nearby. It was too rounded though, and the light rolled to one side and fell to the ground. Instantly the space was plunged into darkness. Clark felt his way around the rocks and stones. They were chilly and damp under his calloused hands.

There was a noise in the far corner. A sort of scraping sound. Clark stopped moving. Listened. But there was only silence now. He felt around the rocks again, moving as quietly as possible so that he wouldn't miss the sound if he heard it again. But there was nothing. Probably a squirrel putting away some nuts for winter.

His hands felt around the crevices, but he still couldn't feel the flashlight. Heat worked its way into his throat. How far could the stupid light have gone? There was only scratchy stone and moist, damp leaves. He continued patting the area and was rewarded with the smooth tip of the flashlight. But only the end of it. The rest must be lodged upside down, inside this crevice between the rocks. He tried to twist his hand, make it smaller. No use. He needed one of the women back here with smaller hands. He considered calling out, asking for help.

Instead, he grabbed at the smooth cylinder once again. He pulled and twisted. No go.

There it was, that noise again. This time it was closer, but still against the far wall. Clark squinted. It was too dark to see anything.

Anger bloomed in his chest. He grabbed at the cylinder again and again. No use. Every time his big fingers slipped off the smooth surface. The heat climbed up from his gut. Everything inside felt hot and red. He should be at Road House Tavern, putting a few beers away and flirting with the girls who ran the joint, not out in the middle of nowhere, wrestling with a …

The noise sounded again. Loud and to his right. Immediately Clark drew his hands in front of his face, fists in tight balls.

Where was it? What was it?

He scuttled back toward the wall. His hip and shoulder bumped against rock.

Again the same strange scraping sound, like fingernails running along a chalkboard's surface.

Closer. Louder.

Clark's breathing sounded ragged in his own ears.

Too-sweet liquid swirled around his teeth. The taste gagged him.

"Thank you," Dell said, putting a hand up to fend off another of Adeline's attempts to spoon hot cocoa into his mouth. "I need a little break." His voice was barely a whisper.

She smiled. "Sure," she said, and put the cup on the ground.

Dell closed his eyes, just for a few seconds. His body was tired, wrung out. He wanted to ask questions but his tongue felt too big for his mouth, fat like when the dentist shot him full of Novocain. He remembered searching in the woods, looking for Alaska.

Where was she?

"Alaska?" he said. The words were so mumbled he could barely hear them. He licked his lips with his giant tongue and tried again.

"Alaska?" This time Adeline heard him. She shook her head.

"No sign yet," she said.

Dell propped himself up on his elbows, the heat of humiliation rising from belly to chest to throat. This was his fault. His doing. If anything happened to his patient …

"Would you like some soup?" Someone across the fire was asking this. He turned his head in that direction, slowly because his neck was stiff and aching. Maria was stirring something steaming in an aluminum pot.

"Not now," he said.

She nodded.

Dell's arms started to tremble. He was as wobbly as a new calf and soon collapsed back onto the sleeping bag beneath him. What he really needed to do was take a leak. The water and cocoa Adeline had been spooning into his mouth was ready to make a second appearance. He sat up again, too fast.

The walls of the cave began to spin. Dell closed his eyes, massaged his temples with a hand. If he could just clear away this fog …

"Where are the others?" he mumbled.

"Clark went to the back to try to get some more branches for the fire," Adeline said. "Gabe is sorting through the supplies."

She'd jerked her head to a spot behind Dell. He nodded but didn't bother to try to see for himself.

"We'll leave in the morning," she said, her voice lower so that only he could hear. "It's too dark to go out tonight. If you're feeling up to it we can break camp at first light. The rain is slowing, maybe it will stop before we head out."

Dell nodded.

"There's something we found, something you might want to look at," she was saying, but Dell had to close his eyes again, lean back on the floor of the cave. He felt like a rag doll, limp and loose. He willed himself to drum up the energy to go back outside and find a private place to urinate.

"Where's Clark?" Maria said. "It shouldn't take that long to gather branches. Do you think he's OK?" Maria looked anxiously from one face to another. Adeline turned from the cave wall and nodded.

"I'm sure he is but maybe I should go check," she said. "He might need help carrying the wood."

She turned and walked toward Gabe and the entrails of the group's packs.

"Can you find me a flashlight?"

He nodded and fumbled through the mess in front of him.

"Here, you are, Doc," he said, handing her the light. She took it. Or rather, she tried to take it. Dell could see Gabe held the other end tightly. The man leaned close and whispered something too low for Dell to hear. Adeline looked startled, then glanced to the back of the cave and back to Gabe. She nodded slowly and stood up to full height. He let go of his grip on the flashlight and Adeline flicked it on and off, making sure that batteries were sound.

What was that all about?

"I'll be back in a few minutes," Adeline said, and started picking her way to the rear of the cave. Dell could see where the room narrowed into a darker space, almost like a hallway. He watched her light moving across the interior and then disappear into the darkness completely.

Chapter Eighteen

The beam of light that bounced around the rocks and crevices made Addie feel a little dizzy. She tried to steady her hand but it was hard. The floors of the cave were jagged and uneven. Her foot would wobble on a rock and she'd pitch one way only to overcorrect and veer in the other direction. The space smelled of earth and rotting leaves and soil that had never seen the sun.

Were there bats in here? She shivered at the thought. Creepy little flying mice. Thoughts of their tiny, jagged teeth and snubbed noses and leathery wings came at her, but she shoved them away. Her hand moved to shine the light toward the ceiling. No. Better not to know. Instead she cast the beam around the walls.

The area she'd entered was narrower than the front where the group was spread out. Here the walls were close. Water gurgled and splashed somewhere further back. Addie shivered, the hair raising on her skin under the long layers.

"Clark?" she called out. "Everything OK?"

The sound of the water was the only reply. Addie moved

in that direction, keeping the flashlight pointed toward the area in front of her feet. Twisting an ankle here could mean a lot of trouble. She heard something, a rasping overhead. Shining the light in that direction, she nearly screamed. Instead she ducked low, covering her head with both arms. The flashlight fell from her hand. A dark flying shape skittered around the area and then flew further back. How many were there?

When she was young her grandmother had told her stories of bats that had gotten tangled in a girl's long hair. The thought made shivers run up her backbone. Addie stooped and retrieved the flashlight which had gone out when she'd dropped it. She clicked the on button. Nothing. Sighing, she flipped the switch off and then on again until a bright stream poured from the end. Much better. Branches were strewn along the sides of the cave and she moved toward them, piling them up for later. Where was he?

"Clark? I came to help you carry back some branches. Do you have a lot?" The word echoed off the rocks and bounced back to her *lot, lot, lot?* Wasn't there a trick about the number of times you heard an echo? A mile for every repeated word or something. One of the boys had told her that.

The water sound was getting much louder. She moved in that direction. The gurgling and splashing noises were changing the further back she walked. Now they were more of a dull roar. Addie frowned, bit her lip. Was there a brook running through the cave? Why hadn't Gabe mentioned that? He was the only one who'd been back here. She thought about what the artist had told her, that she should watch out for the creature with the golden eyes. Was he trying to scare her?

And where was Clark? How far back did this cave go? Had he lost his way? Maybe his flashlight had died and he'd stumbled in the wrong direction. Toward the water. But that didn't make any sense. Why go toward the sound of roaring water if you can't see anything?

Addie looked back the way she'd come. It was dark, too. The light from the fire was far behind her, too far to see. She took several more steps, then paused again to listen. The water sounds were coming from her left. She shone the light around again. The area had gotten wider, the walls opening up slightly. To the right was a huge boulder. Beside it was a large pile of smaller stones. The left artery of the cave was wide. Did it narrow beyond where the beam of light shone?

A sudden thought jolted Addie. Where were the sticks and branches that Clark had gathered? If something had happened, wouldn't he have dropped them? And if he hadn't been collecting them, what was he doing back here?

Maria stirred the soup in the thin aluminum pot. Everything happening was surreal: the trip itself, Alaska getting lost, taking shelter in this freak storm. And not just any shelter, this creepy place with the weird drawings ... Her eyes went to the ceiling automatically. Were they really just some teenagers' idea of a prank? They looked authentic, old. But who could tell in this dim light? She wished there was a spotlight that she could shine up there, illuminating the entire ceiling.

Gabe coughed and Maria glanced over. He was repacking

the backpacks that were left: three, not counting Alaska's, Addie's or Dr. O'Dell's. Someone still needed to go back out into the rain and find that one. She glanced at Dr. O'Dell, imagining he'd be sleeping again. Maria had never known that hypothermia could do that to a person, make them so weak and confused. It hadn't even seemed all that cold out. She'd always assumed hypothermia was something that was only a danger in the arctic, or a snowstorm or something.

Maria glanced at Gabe again. He was staring at her, still whistling a creepy little tune. Or maybe it only seemed creepy because he was doing it so slowly and the notes were bouncing off the stone. "Three Blind Mice," wasn't it? She hadn't heard it since kindergarten. It was an awful rhyme, too; she'd always hated it.

"Staying hydrated?" Gabe asked. The pause in the music was abrupt. Maria sat in the silence a moment before answering.

"Yes. I had water and some of the soup. Did you want any? There's plenty left." She nodded to the pot. The steam wavered in the air between them. It was a dehydrated meal and left a strange metallic aftertaste in Maria's mouth. Or maybe it was the pot that did that. Anyway, it was hot and felt good in her stomach.

"Sure," Gabe said. "That sounds great. I think the packs are all set now. I distributed the food evenly between each one if you want to double-check my work." He smiled.

She smiled back but it was forced. "No, I'm sure it's fine," she said.

Pouring the hot soup into the metal cup that Gabe held

out she concentrated on not spilling any of the liquid on her hand or Gabe's. The cup shook a little in his hands.

"That's good," he said, pulling the cup away. "Thanks."

"You're welcome," Maria said. She poured a little more into her cup, then put the pot to the side of the fire, nestled it on some rocks then turned to look at Dr. O'Dell. He was white and pasty but breathing evenly. That was good, she guessed.

"Camp a lot?" Gabe asked.

Maria shook her head.

"No. This is my first time, since I was a kid I mean."

"Right. All kids camp, don't they?" Gabe asked.

Maria smiled. "Probably. It seems that way."

"Did you camp with your family or …?" he let the rest of the question linger in the air while he blew into the soup, trying to cool it off.

"No. My family isn't really into nature. I went with friends from school. Nothing like this though, just campgrounds."

"Really? You've never been to summer camp?"

"No, never."

"You sure? Lake Bomoseen is down in the southern part of the state. Ever heard of it?"

Maria shrugged. "I don't think so."

"I went to a summer camp there for years. My grandparents thought it would toughen me up. I was an only child and they worried that I spent too much time alone. I went every summer until the eighth grade. What age are you then, fourteen?"

Maria smiled and nodded.

"It didn't do much for me. Honestly, I don't really like being in nature a whole lot, I'd rather be in the studio. Are you sure you didn't go? 'Cause you look really familiar."

Maria shook her head again, and stirred the soup. She took a sip trying to look somewhere other than Gabe's eyes which were pinned on her. It tasted slightly sour in her mouth.

"It was a long time ago. But I remember one summer in particular. Actually, it was the last one that I went. There were three friends there, and I would have sworn one of them was you, Maria. You could be twins." He said this with a laugh, but it sounded harsh and forced.

"Hmm," was all Maria said and stared into the fire. She could feel his eyes on her and fear skittered up her backbone. She glanced at Dr. O'Dell again, but he was asleep, his mouth slightly open, a whistle coming out each time he released a breath. Where were the others?

"… yeah, she looked just like you. She was a real bitch." His voice had grown hard. "Her and her friends played a nasty trick on me."

Maria looked at him again, her heartbeat pounding in her chest, her hands shaking around the cup of hot liquid. He was still staring at her, the firelight casting shadows along the planes of his homely face. But there was something else that stopped her breath in her chest. A shadow stood behind Gabe, undulating and beginning to form a shape. A weird scraping, scratching sound filled the cave. The shadow moved and twisted into the shape of a man. Maria closed her eyes and then opened them again. Surely she was imagining it?

The shadow was still there, bending now toward Gabe. The grating sounds grew louder.

Maria pointed at it, the cup of hot soup falling from her hand and splashing on the rocks near the fire.

Gabe smiled at her and then cocked his head as though listening to something the shadow man was telling him. Maria listened too, but all she could hear was the scratching and clicking, and the wind howling outside the cave's entrance.

"I'm sorry," Gabe said to her, then stood. The shadow moved behind him, pressing closer. Its form bled around the edges, little tendrils of black smoke dissipating into the air around Gabe. It had gotten cold, too, as though the thing brought icy air with it.

"Wh-what?" was all Maria could say. Her lips felt numb. She stood as well, legs shaking.

"I'm sorry to do this to you, Maria, or should I say Tiffany?"

"No, I'm not—"

But before she could get the rest of the words out, Gabe was moving toward her. He lurched suddenly and she thought he'd fallen. But then he righted himself and she could see a rock in his hand, large and jagged looking.

He's going to kill me.

Maria screamed and the sound bounced around the walls of the cave. Then Gabe lunged toward her and his face changed from smiling that strange, ugly smile, to a snarl.

Chapter Nineteen

Addie looked down the side of the ravine, her breath ragged in her throat. This was where the water sounds were coming from. The cave continued though, pressing even further back. Had Clark slipped down this steep bank of rock into the water below? Or maybe he'd gone out the back entrance, circled around like Gabe. He could be sitting by the fire right now, stacking up a pile of branches and sipping cocoa and broth with the others. Should she go back? Her legs and arms and back screamed yes. But what if he was here somewhere, hurt?

Addie peeked over the side again and let out a long, slow sigh. Climbing down into the ravine was reckless, stupid. If she fell, then what? Who would come to rescue her? She should go back to camp, get Gabe and some rope. "What if it was one of your boys down there?" A little voice asked from the back of her mind. "Would you wait then?"

Grumbling, Addie set the flashlight down on the ground, making sure it wasn't going to roll off the edge. Then she sat, scooted her butt to the edge of the ravine and started lowering herself down, making sure her feet stayed in contact with the side. It was dirty and damp but not steep enough that she would fall, if she was careful. And if her feet didn't lose their grip on the dirt and small stones. She turned her body so that now she was facing the side of the cave wall and grabbed the flashlight. She tried to hold it with one hand but it was impossible to move without both hands free. Stowing it in her bra, light pointed upward, she slowly eased her way down, using rocks and boulders as hand and footholds.

The deeper she went, the louder the water sound became and the moister the air got. Addie turned after several minutes and leaned against a boulder, catching her breath and resting her legs. She pulled the flashlight free and shone it around beneath her.

There were rocks, rocks and more rocks. But she could also just see the stream or river or whatever it was just beyond another outcropping of stones. Slowly, she panned the light from left to right, as far as the beam would go. There! What was that?

A pale flash of white against another section of rocks, further down and to her right. Was it a hand? Addie scrambled down the rest of the way, not bothering to be as careful with where she put her feet. Her heartbeat banged away, her breathing heavier.

"Clark?" The words were barely audible over the sound of the rushing water. "Claaaark?" she shouted.

Scooting across a large, flat boulder, she shone the light over the pale splotch. Her gasp was louder than even the roar of the water. It wasn't Clark's hand, but a skeleton's.

Light pushed against Dell's eyelids. He moved his head, trying to block it out. No luck. Had he forgotten to close the curtains before bed? Pulling an arm over his eyes, he dipped back into unconsciousness. A sound woke him minutes later. What was it? Something unfamiliar, out of place in his bedroom. A kitten meowing maybe.

Dell moved his arm and opened his eyes. The light wasn't coming in through the window across from his king-sized bed but from a fire. It burned brightly in the dim light of the cave. The cave. Everything came rushing back and he sat up suddenly. The walls around him moved slightly and he put a hand up, massaged his temples. The trip. The cave. The group. But where was everyone?

Dell looked around, more slowly this time. The fire was glowing and nearby was a stack of backpacks. But no people.

"Hello?" he called out, his voice weak. "Where is everyone?"

There was that sound again. A little animal whimpering. Dell pulled himself out of the sleeping bag, shoved his legs into the damp pair of pants nearby and pulled on his boots. They were still crusted with mud and the insides were slightly squishy. He didn't bother tying the laces but did pull on the shirt that was nearly dry from the fire. Immediately, he started to shiver, but ignored the cold and followed the sound. It was coming from the mouth of the cave. He walked more quickly, steadying himself momentarily on rocks when the dizziness returned.

He heard the noise again. More loudly. He picked up his

pace, then tripped and nearly fell. Righting himself he moved to the edge of the opening and poked his head outside. Maria was sprawled on the ground. One leg was twisted at a strange angle.

"What happened?" Dell asked, rushing to her side. The young woman sobbed in response.

"Please, get me out of here. He's going to come back any second."

"Who?"

"Please, just help me up."

"I think your leg might be broken," Dell said, but started to turn the woman over onto her back. "Can you get your arm around my shoulders?"

She nodded but her arm didn't move.

"I'm sorry. I can't move very well. I need to get out of here. He might come back any minute. Please," she said, looking wildly around the woods near Dell.

"Who? What are you talking … here, we'll get you up. Don't worry. Everything is going to be fine."

She sobbed again. Dell stooped further into a squat, pulled her arm across his shoulders and stood. Or tried to. He was still wobbly.

"Let's try again. Ready?"

She nodded.

Dell resumed his original position. This time they made it upright and he started to walk back toward the cave.

"Hurry. He's coming back. We need to find something, a weapon."

"Who, Maria? Who's coming back?" Dell grunted. His

legs still felt noodle-ish. They were nearly to the cave door.

"Gabe. He wants to kill me."

"What?" Dell's voice sounded incredulous in his own ears. He paused to readjust Maria's arm. Their damp skin only made it more difficult to hold onto her.

"Just keep going," Maria said, then gasped in pain when Dell stumbled on a stone. "We need to find some way to protect ourselves."

Dell wanted to tell Maria that she must be hallucinating. Gabe suffered from panic disorder and stress-related anxiety. He was a far cry from violent. But he didn't say anything. Talking at the present moment took up too much energy.

They got through the mouth of the cave and slowly picked their way across the stones and uneven ground. Maria cried out twice—gasping, *my leg, my leg*—and Dell slowed enough to readjust her position. Finally, he got them to the fire and gently helped her onto his sleeping bag.

"Stay right here. I'm just going to find a stick we can use to keep your leg straight." Maria whimpered in response. Her eyes were closed and Dell could see thin trails of dried tears on her cheeks become wet again.

"Be careful," she said. "He's out there. He only ran off when he saw, when he saw—" Maria's voice broke off and a shudder ran through her body. "When he saw the creature. The one Alaska saw. It's real, Dr. O'Dell."

Chapter Twenty

Shining her flashlight outward, Addie tried to catch her breath. Maybe it was an animal's skeleton. The water gurgled and tumbled over rocks and along hidden pockets in the silt underneath the surface. Further down, to the right, the sound of moving water was much, much louder, but here the water was gentler. She took another deep breath, then one more and shone the light back to the bones near her feet.

No, these were human bones. Her hand went to her mouth automatically, but then she recoiled, tasting and smelling the mud and moss and God knew what else embedded on her palms.

The box that Gabe found and the papers inside. Was this the remains of one of the missing people? Or the skeleton of the woman who'd written the journal pages? She bent down, careful not to disturb the spot with her boots or to touch anything. She had no idea what she was looking for, other than to try to determine if the bones had belonged to a man or a woman. For some reason, it felt important to know. There was a ring on the ring finger of the left hand, she could see. It flopped loosely there, against the joint. The body was twisted unnaturally, with most of the ribs crushed and broken; the whole frame looked as though it was curled around a large boulder nearby. Had someone been hiking here and fallen? Or been hiding?

A noise cut through the roar of the water and Addie jumped, nearly dropping the light. She whirled around toward the sound. It had been loud, a scraping sound. Something moving along the rocks? Like something metallic moving over stone … But there was nothing there. Heart pounding, she skimmed the flashlight's beam over rocks and crevices.

No movement. No other sounds.

Then the light caught something. Something shiny and golden-colored. Something that looked like golden eyes. The flashlight dimmed, the bright light becoming yellowed. Addie swore and shook it. The light went out altogether. Addie backed up, whacking the flashlight against her thigh. She took a step back, then another. *Whack, whack, whack,* she smacked the flashlight on her leg. It stung.

No luck.

She heard a different sound now, something between a groan and rumble. Then the grating sound once more.

Whack, whack. Finally, the light turned back on. She immediately shone it toward the spot where she'd seen the golden eyes. There was nothing there.

Dell paced a narrow space on the floor of the cave where there were no rocks. Back and forth, back and forth.

Occasionally he glanced at Maria. She'd passed out while he was positioning the makeshift splint. Her leg was broken, about halfway down the big bone of the leg. The femur. It was the largest bone in the human body. Right? He still felt a little disoriented. A little foggy.

How had she broken it? And what had she meant about Gabe? She was hallucinating most likely. She'd mumbled other things that hadn't made sense while he'd worked on the splint, things about swimming in the rain and camps and golden eyes. But where was Gabe? And where were Clark and Adeline?

Dell stopped pacing and rubbed his hands over his face. He needed to go and look for the others, needed to return to the woods and find his pack, but he couldn't leave an injured woman here all alone. What if a wild animal came to the cave to seek shelter from the storm? What if …

The packs. They'd left them here, in the front of the cave but the food should all be up in the trees. It was the first rule of overnight hiking. Never leave food in your tent or around your camp. It would draw wild animals, especially bear. It was October but not too late in the season for bears to still be preparing themselves for hibernation in caves just like this one.

He glanced at the sleeping woman and then at the packs. They were down to two now: Clark's and Maria's; Gabe must have taken his with him. After one of the others came back he'd go out and try to find his own. Walking to the pile, he pulled the zipper open on Maria's backpack and rummaged around until he found what he was looking for.

A long length of rope, a nylon stuff sack. Now he just needed the food. His hands unearthed everything but: pots, collapsible water jug, first aid kit, more clothing, candles and matches.

No food.

Frantically, he dumped the pack upside down and shook it. He pawed through the contents, carefully at first, then more frantically.

The food was gone. Surely they couldn't have eaten everything already? How long had he been unconscious?

He searched Clark's pack next. There, at the bottom of the pack he heard the crinkling of food wrappers. He sorted through the plastic zipped bags. There were a few dehydrated soups, two emergency meals in foil packets, two candy bars. That was it.

Dell sat back on his haunches. He'd heard someone, maybe Adeline, asking Gabe what he'd been doing with the food. If he'd been the one sorting it, then he'd taken it all for himself, save what little was left in Clark's pack.

Thunder boomed outside and Dell groaned. Not again. Not more. He had to hurry. Get the food up in the tree before the rain started coming down hard again. He replaced the contents of each pack minus the food. Next, he collected a small pile of rocks then put them into the nylon stuff sack. These would act as the counter weight while he tried to get the back up and over a sturdy tree branch. Satisfied it was heavy enough without being too hard to throw, Dell pulled on a rain jacket and filled the pockets with what food was left.

Outside, the rain was picking up again. It fell more softly than earlier, dripping off leaves and tree branches lazily. The torrents had slowed but the ground was still squishy and soft. Dell watched where he walked, careful to stay where there was more foliage and undergrowth. He tied a length of rope to the stuff sack and tossed it over a tree branch yards from camp. It should be a hundred yards but Dell was too tired to count it out.

He threw the nylon bag into the air. It sailed up and fell back to the ground without crossing the branch. Dell sighed and did it again. And again. His arms and legs felt heavy, his head pounded.

On the sixth try, the small sack swung over the branch. Dell rushed forward. He adjusted the rope in his hand, letting the sack come down to belly-height. Then he opened it, removed the rocks and replaced them with the food from his pockets. Carefully he knotted the end around the bag then pulled and pulled until the bag swung up into the air. He gauged the height and pulled some more.

When the pack was more than twelve feet from the ground, Dell stopped. He rested against the tree for a few seconds, water dripping onto his coat and running down his neck.

Then he knotted the rope to the lowest tree branch three times. Tomorrow he'd repeat the process in reverse, pull the food down and they could all share it, prepare for the hike out. A coyote yipped far off. Its keening voice was followed by another and another.

Chapter Twenty-One

Addie's heart slammed in her chest, her breaths came in gasps. She could feel the golden eyes pinning her, could hear the rasping, grating sound of claws on stones as that thing—whatever it was—caught up to her. She could almost hear the ragged breath of it in her wake. Feel its hot breath on her ankles …

She purposefully slowed her stride, nowhere close to stopping but making each movement a little bit more focused and a little bit less frantic. That thing—whatever it was—was not coming after her. It was long gone. She used to tell the boys that when they were small. They'd be lying in the tent after dark, whispering about the strange sounds outside the thin nylon walls.

"What's that, Mama?" Ben would ask her again and again.

"It's probably just a raccoon or an opossum," she'd say. "It's already moved on, Ben. Try to go to sleep now."

Her lips, parted now for more air, twisted slightly. God, how she wished Ben and Michael were here. Addie's foot slipped on a damp stone and she went down on one knee. Pain radiated up the front of her thigh and she bit back a yell of pain and frustration. Part of her just wanted to stay on the ground, sit and rest for a few minutes. But she pushed herself upward, rubbing her knee and testing her weight on it gently. It was OK. She hadn't broken anything.

Scrambling up the last few feet, Addie was once again on the lip of the ravine. She turned now; with her flashlight she scanned the area she'd just climbed. No hulking beast loomed, no creature with gold eyes stared back. Addie's fingers were trembling as she pushed loose pieces of hair back behind her ears.

Then something clamped onto her right shoulder.

Dell had gotten back into the cave with seconds to spare. A torrential downpour had restarted outside. He stood, watching the rain for a few minutes. The food should stay dry, even with all the water cascading downward. He hadn't gotten the pack quite as far from camp as he should have, but doubted a bear would seek it out in the storm.

A noise broke the relative quiet, coming from the back of the cave. He listened, willing the rain to be quiet. Nothing. Turning, he looked toward the fire and Maria. She still appeared to be sleeping, her head wedged up on a makeshift pillow—someone's dry pair of extra pants. The firelight made shadows dance on the walls behind her.

Dell started toward the rear of the cave. She would be okay here for a few minutes. Just while he checked out the noise. He walked slowly, using a large branch that had been leaning on the wall of the cave as a walking stick. It helped. Gave him balance and felt good and heavy in his hand. In a pinch, he'd use it as a weapon.

What had happened to the gun? He always brought it along when he went on trips like this. He was certain he'd packed it. In the little nylon case. Who …

Dell's heart leapt in his chest as a scream cut through the air. He ran, stumbling over loose stones and nearly falling once on a rock that was jutting out. The flashlight beam bounced with every step, creating weird shadows and movement on the walls.

"Adeline?" he called out. "Adeline?"

As soon as he said her name, he regretted it. If she was being attacked then surprise would have been his best weapon. Too late now. He followed the cave wall to the spot where it narrowed, shone his beam down the tunnel-like enclosure. Immediately he felt like he was five years old again, at the bottom of that well. The tunnel ahead loomed dark and close, the walls damp and musty smelling. Dell swallowed once. Twice. Then holding the branch upright like a sword, he walked deeper into the cave.

The sound of water, rushing water, was louder here. The rain that had been pouring down must be feeding this brook. There was a faint aroma of bat guano mixed with the dank smell of wet rocks. Dell turned the flashlight to the left, then the right, scanning the area.

"Dell?" Adeline's voice called out. Immediately, he swung the beam in that direction.

"Where are you?" he called.

Before the sentence had left his lips though, he saw her. She stood, hunched over and small looking. He rushed to her side, kicking a few small rocks in the process. They scattered and bounced over the ground. She turned to him, putting a hand up protectively against the light. He moved the beam, sweeping it over the area.

"Clark?"

The big man was sitting nearby on a rock, head between his hands.

"Are you injured?" Dell asked Adeline, drawing close enough to smooth her hair away from her face. Her cheeks and forehead were smudged with dirt. She was shivering.

"Not me, but Clark. I'm not sure what's wrong. I found him when I climbed up," she turned, pointed over her shoulder to a steep drop off that Dell hadn't known was there. "He grabbed my shoulder which is when I yelled. But he doesn't seem … I don't know. Right," she said. "It's like he's in a trance or something."

Dell moved toward his client. The man was sitting on a big stone, cradling his head in his hands and rocking back and forth.

"There's something else," Adeline said through chattering teeth. Dell handed her the flashlight which she promptly dropped. She picked it up and leaning over, he almost missed her next words.

"I think I saw … the thing that Alaska saw. And there is a skeleton," she nodded back toward the ravine. "Down there."

"One thing at a time," Dell said. "Let's get you and Clark back to camp. Maria has been hurt."

"She's hurt? Oh no." Then, "Where's Gabe?"

Dell shook his head. "I'm not sure."

"Clark," he asked, turning. "Can you walk?"

No response.

"Clark?"

Dell sighed, rubbed a hand over his face, under his eyes, squeezing at the pressure that had built there over the past hour.

"Can you walk?" he asked Adeline.

"Yes, of course. I can help you with Clark."

"No, I'll get him. Take my flashlight and lead the way with the light."

Adeline nodded.

"Clark, I need you to stand up now," Dell said, walking toward the bigger man. He touched his arm.

Clark sprang upward, his face twisted, a growl escaping his mouth. His right hand shot forward, grabbing at Dell's throat.

Dell gasped in surprise. Then the hand started to squeeze and he was choking. He couldn't breathe. Dell couldn't see anything but bright firework bursts exploding in front of his eyes. The edges of his vision were black. He tried to turn his head, to look at Adeline. To beg her, *please, don't leave me in the dark*. But no words would come.

Chapter Twenty-Two

"Stop it! Let go, you're hurting him," Addie yelled, the sound bouncing around the rocks and stone walls. She pummeled Clark's arms. They felt like unyielding chunks of wood under her fists. Stepping backward, she ducked low and plowed into him. The man grunted in response, then teetered. A burning pain coursed down the side of Addie's neck and she put a hand to the left side, supporting it as she looked upward. From her awkward angle she could see Clark wobbling, his grip on Dell lost. She stumbled to her feet at the same time that Dell stumbled backward.

"Are you OK?" she asked, supporting him slightly with her body. He nodded.

"Fine," he said. His voice was little more than a croak.

"Clark?" Addie called out. The man was sitting once again on a large stone. Instead of his head in his hands though, they hung limply at his sides. He was staring at the floor. His chest rose and fell quickly. Addie cautiously moved closer.

"Clark, what is going on," she asked. "Are you sick?"

Clark didn't answer. He sat motionless for a few seconds then looked up. His eyes were strange, the muted light in the area making them appear to glow.

"Clark." She put a hand on one of his. "Are you sick?" she repeated.

He motioned with the free hand to his mouth. He couldn't talk? Maybe he was going to vomit.

"Are you nauseous?"

The man continued to stare at her. He didn't blink. She glanced back at Dell who appeared to be in a trance. He was staring off into the deep recesses of the cave, his hands still trembling.

Clark was finally moving. He motioned to her to come closer. She did, barely. He motioned again, then, opened his mouth. It wasn't the kind of opening you do at the dentist. Instead, barely perceptibly, his lower jaw began to drop open. It opened wider and wider. Too wide, until his chin grazed his chest.

Inside, his mouth was hollow. Clark's tongue was gone.

"You don't just lose a tongue," Dell said. They were back at the makeshift camp. The fire was burning very low. They'd need more wood if they wanted to keep it going the rest of the night, Addie thought distractedly. Or maybe they should leave now.

She refocused on Dell. What was he saying?

"And it's not possible that something attacked him. There would be signs of that—blood and lots of it. What the hell is happening?" he said, his voice ending with a crack like an adolescent's. "This just can't be—"

"We need to stay calm and regroup," Addie said. Her voice was firm, sounded so normal and level-headed.

"And Clark?"

"Clark—" inappropriate phrases flooded her brain: "he won't be wagging his tongue" and "his tongue lashings are over." Addie rubbed her fingertips over her forehead, massaging her temples.

"I need some water," she said, and moved toward the packs.

"But what about Clark?" Dell's voice was a loud whisper, following her.

When had she become trip leader? Anger burned Addie's esophagus. This wasn't her idea, these weren't her problems. She wanted to yell and scream and fall into a heap on the floor crying. Dell stood hunched, his arms dangling by his legs, as though they didn't have any strength left. Addie felt the anger drain away. He looked so lost, so, fragile.

"There's nothing we can do to help him right now," she said calmly. "I don't know what happened—we'll figure it out later. But if we don't get ourselves together, start thinking straight, there won't be a later."

The words seemed to have an effect on Dell. He straightened to his full height, shook his head as though to clear it.

"You're right, of course," he said. He cleared his throat. "We have to put what's happened to Clark away for the moment and figure out how to get safely back to ..." his voice drifted for a moment. "Back home."

Home. The word caused so much longing that Addie

turned away from Dell. Images of her cozy kitchen flooded her mind despite her best attempts to hold them back: the smell of cinnamon and cloves—she liked to mix these with water and let them simmer on a back burner—the way the light slanted through the window in the breakfast nook, catching on the blue glass bottles she'd collected since she was a girl. Her two boys gathered around the table, ready to eat.

Addie let out a shaky breath. She had to stop this. Now. Taking a deep breath, she turned, searching the packs for water. Two collapsible jugs were half-filled. Addie grabbed at the first one and unscrewed the cap, tipping it up to her lips and drinking.

"How's Maria," she asked, looking to the young woman in the sleeping bag.

"She's fine," Dell said. "Despite her broken leg."

Addie sat close to the fire, drawing up her knees. Her boot banged into something with a clang. The metal box. She'd forgotten all about it when everything happened with Clark. She put it on her lap.

"What's that?" Dell asked.

"Gabe found it in the back part of the cave when he went to collect branches."

"May I?"

Addie handed the box to him wordlessly. She was quiet while he read, all the aches and scrapes reminding her that she shouldn't have stopped moving, shouldn't have sat down. But her bones were tired. Just a few minutes wouldn't hurt, would it?

Dell read in silence for few minutes, then made a noise under his breath before carefully depositing the papers back into their thick envelope and returning the packet to the tin. Addie watched him as she wiped the dampness from her face with the hem of her shirt.

"What do you think?" she said, finally.

"Old wives' tales, most likely. Or the imagination of people with nothing better to do."

"I saw it, Dell."

His eyes widened and he looked at her with surprise edging his face.

"Saw it?"

"That thing, that creature. It was the same one with golden eyes that Alaska saw in the woods. It was standing. Not walking on all fours, but standing up, taller than you. It was down at the bottom of the ravine."

Dell was silent a moment. Then, "You shouldn't have gone down there alone. You could have been seriously hurt and then what? No one even knew where you were."

They were both silent for a few long moments, staring into the flames.

"Are you sure of what you saw?" Dell asked.

Addie nodded. "Positive."

He didn't say anything else, just rubbed a hand over his jaw.

"I'd like to see it," he said. "And the skeleton. We could hike back down if you're up for it."

Addie nodded. She was exhausted but the thought of finding out more about the creature, of Dell seeing it and verifying what she'd seen, was exhilarating.

"Yes let's," she said.

"First though, I need to go and retrieve my pack. In all the excitement," he turned away from Clark now, looking back to Addie, "I forgot about it. But there are more supplies in there, and we may need them. You should get some sleep," he said, motioning toward the fire where Maria lay. "At least for a few minutes."

"I couldn't sleep now if I tried," Addie said.

"Still, you should give it a go," Dell responded.

Addie nodded. "I'll try."

Dell asked her where she'd found him and she did her best to explain, then sat down by the fire, on the opposite side as Maria. Clark seemed to have fallen asleep sitting up, his head nodding to his chest.

Suddenly, Addie's eyelids felt too heavy to hold up. Behind the lids though, jumpy pictures of everything that had happened the last two days danced incessantly. She opened her eyes and looked around. Nothing was out of place, no shadows other than the ones created by the fire.

Then she felt it. Warm, wetness dripped onto her face and ran down her neck. Putting a hand there, Addie gasped when she pulled it away. It was covered in blood.

Chapter Twenty-Three

"Cave walls do this sometimes," Dell said. He'd returned with his pack, victorious, twenty minutes after he left.

"It's likely the beginning of a dripstone." He glanced at Adeline. "It's how stalactites form. Though usually those are in the deeper recesses."

"Are they normally red like this?"

Dell shook his head. "I think the color is coming from that," he pointed upward to the strange drawings and symbols on the cave's ceiling. Adeline's eyes followed his finger. She shook her head.

"I can't wait to get out of here."

"Should we go to the ravine now, while they're both sleeping?"

Adeline nodded. Dell could see a sort of nervous energy fueling her. Her eyes were sharp and clear, even after all they'd been through in the last twenty-four hours. He had been right to ask her along. For all that had gone wrong on this trip, he was grateful that she was here with them, part of this group.

"Let's go," he said and hoisted his pack. Adeline followed.

"Did you know that caves have long been associated with the supernatural?" he asked. If Adeline answered he couldn't hear. "From as far back as prehistoric times, some say, and at least as far back as the time when Greece was a powerful entity. People often traveled to caves to seek spiritual enlightenment, or some would say, to communicate with the spirits themselves."

"The only person I want to communicate with is a rescue unit," Adeline said loudly enough to be heard over the rumbling of the water beneath them.

Dell smiled.

"Tell me more," Adeline said. "It's taking my mind off of what's down there."

Dell felt relief bloom in his gut. Finally, he could do something helpful. He searched his mind for more information on caves. "Native Americans often used caves as places to find enlightenment of some sorts. The Lakota tribe actually believed that a certain cave in the Black Hills was the spot of the creation of humankind."

"Really?"

"Yes. Caves are a place of mystery and untapped wonders to many. They are like the deepest depths of the sea— unexplored areas where many adventurers look for the hidden secrets of the past."

"Have you been in this one before?"

"No."

"I used to explore the caves behind my house when I was a kid," Adeline said. "But they were longer and narrower than this. There were little rooms; well, alcoves in the rock really. Supposedly they were used during Prohibition for rum running."

"Is that so?" Dell asked. "Have you ever been to the caves at Smuggler's Notch?"

He thought he heard a yes from behind him. "Those were used during Prohibition too. Though I think there were cows smuggled in them too, not just booze."

"Cows? Why?"

Before Dell could answer he heard a gasp from behind him.

"Bats!" Adeline squealed.

Dell looked up, moving his flashlight above him. A large brown bat flew erratically toward his face. Instinctively, he put his hands up, dropping the light in the process. He felt a feathery wing touch his cheek and another near his hand.

"Where's the light? The light, Dell, where's the light?" Her voice had risen two octaves, and was close to his ear. He felt her fingers on his shoulder, then one gripping his side. They dug in and he had to hold back an exclamation of pain. He dropped to a squat, every muscle in his body screeching, and groped around on the floor with one hand, keeping the other in front of his face. He wasn't scared of bats—they weren't really the blood-sucking vampires that most people believed them to be—but they would bite if they felt threatened.

"Just a minute," he said in his most soothing therapy voice. "I almost have it, Adeline."

He found the light and shone it around above them. The colony had moved on.

"Probably going out for their night of feeding," he remarked.

Adeline didn't respond but he heard a whoosh of breath, and then her fingers released her grip. Even though it hadn't been comfortable, he missed her touch.

"I thought they hibernated," she said, her voice growing louder as the sound of rushing water filled the space around them.

"Some do," he shouted over his shoulder. Then, "Is this it?"

They stood at the top of a ravine. Adeline shouted back over the rushing below.

"Yes. Follow me down," she said. "Can I have the light?"

Dell nodded, handing it to her. He forced a smile but underneath his skin was starting to crawl. The walls of the cave pressed in closer. Damp and smothering. No matter how much Adeline disliked bats there was no way it was as much as Dell hated enclosed spaces. Dark, enclosed spaces.

Adeline turned and started down. "Watch yourself on the rocks. They're more slippery the further down you get." Dell paused for a moment, taking a couple of deep breaths and imagining his own fears flying away like the furry flying rodents. It didn't work.

Several minutes later they'd reached the bottom of the ravine. Adeline moved closer to the sound of the water which was even louder here. He followed the light blindly. What if she lost it? What if the batteries died? They'd left the extra one with Maria and Clark, in case … in case of what? It was a stupid decision. The two were practically comatose. Why would they need a flashlight?

Adeline stopped abruptly and Dell ran into her. She made a soft, "ugh" sound.

"Sorry," he yelled above the roar of the water. "Do you see something?" He looked around, trying to see ahead of Adeline, trying to get his bearings.

Adeline was shaking her head. At least, that's what Dell thought at first. Then he saw the tremble take over the beam of the flashlight. Her arms were shaking too. Dell put a steadying hand on her shoulder. He felt tremors passing through her entire body.

"Adeline? What is it? You're …"

His words died away while his mind tried to understand exactly what he was seeing. He blinked, would have rubbed his eyes but he didn't dare move a finger. This couldn't be … there was no way …

Before them stood the creature that the women had seen. Dark colored, covered in hair. It stood on two legs like a man, just like Adeline had said. Was it a man? David couldn't make out any features. It was tall, too. Seven feet? Eight? The head was turned away from them, looking down and back. Its hands hung limply on the end of overly-long arms. Adeline made a noise that sounded like she was strangling. Without thinking, Dell clamped a hand over her mouth.

Too late. The thing swung its head in their direction.

Dell started retreating, backing up one unsteady step at a time, pulling Adeline along with him. His heart slammed into his ribcage. His breath was fast and loud out of his mouth. Images raced through his mind, a jumble of past and present snapshots: staring up from the darkness at the bright light above from the old well; Clark's open mouth void of tongue; the spiders and webs that had tangled in his curls as a child; Adeline's frantic expression; the sight of the creature. It had been turned away, headed in a different direction. But now the golden eyes stared at them.

"Get out of here," Dell said, his mouth close to Adeline's ear. "Now."

She was in a trance. Her eyes were pinned on the beast or man; whatever it was. Dell reached around her, slowly, lowered the flashlight from the creature's face. He could feel her trembling and shaking, even harder than before.

Then it moved toward them. Without even a glance at the floor studded with rocks and chunks of broken boulders, it moved effortlessly. Almost gracefully. Dell pulled Adeline, turning her around so that she was facing the other direction. Then he shoved her.

"Run," he yelled.

Chapter Twenty-Four

Maria heard kids laughing. The notes tumbled over one another, bubbles of innocence. She smiled, leaning back against the old maple tree. The leaves above whispered as they moved in an invisible breeze. The sun was warm on her face, the smell of fresh greenness and new beginnings all around her.

Then a stick poked her leg. She frowned, readjusted her position. But it was there again. Poking her. She moved a hand to brush it away but the pain became more intense, sharp and hot. Maria wiggled again, trying to move her leg away from whatever it was that was hurting it. The pain only followed. Anger bubbled suddenly in her chest. Such a beautiful day! Spoiled by this stupid branch. She moved her hand down her leg more gently this time, exploring. Heat radiated up from her thigh into her hand. Why was her skin so hot? Burning.

Suddenly Maria realized how thirsty she was. Her throat was nearly raw with it. She turned her head, looking over the landscape for water. But there was none. The trees above, green and lush, began to turn brittle and dry. The sun, no longer dappled by the canopy of green leaves, fell onto her, drifting down in tiny piles of ash.

The children had stopped laughing and in the silence Maria heard something else: a dull, roaring sound. A train? No, something else. She searched her mind for the right noise but her brain felt slow and stupid. Too hot. She couldn't think straight. Water. Where could she find water?

Another sound filled the space. Something strange and garbled. It sounded like, *aahhhhgggaaa.* The pain in her leg intensified the hotter she became. Now it felt as though someone were sticking a poker into her flesh, a hot poker between the muscle and bone, prying it apart.

Please, water. She tried to make her lips form the words but they were too sticky, like hot candle wax. *Water.*

Aahhhgggaaaa. The sound again. Was it human? Maria turned her head to the right and then the left, scanning the brown horizon. Dead trees with bare branches framed a field with charred grass. The heat pressed in on her, came in waves like ocean water. The tree behind her was suddenly scratchy and rough, pressing its bark sharply into her shoulder bones and spine. She craned her neck, looking behind her. There was something there … something she couldn't see.

A brown figure walked toward her. Tall and covered in a black suit. An astronaut's suit but without the helmet. Like a hood or a winter toque pulled down over its face. It was dark too, like the rest of the suit. It moved gracefully, as though the cumbersome suit was its second skin.

Skin. Maria's felt like it was on fire. The closer the

creature got, the hotter she felt. Maria moaned, tried to turn her head away but it was pinned to the tree. Stuck in place. Melted? She cried out—tried to. But her lips had stopped working. The figure was drawing nearer. Maria wanted to close her eyes, to look away. But she couldn't. She was stuck. A pile of gooey, warm tar.

Closer it came. Closer. Then Maria saw. It wasn't a suit at all but a body, huge and covered with fur. Too-long arms hung loosely by the creature's sides. Its golden eyes glowed from the dark face.

Maria opened her mouth to scream. But she was a pile of wax and wax didn't move.

Clark moved his hands under the young woman's head. She was hot. Too hot. Fever, maybe. He felt so tired. It had taken long minutes to rouse himself enough to crawl to her side. She was moaning, her head moved side to side.

Medicine?

Clark looked around slowly. The space moved with him, walls undulating in and out. He put both hands over his head until the spinning stopped.

"Don't you ever get tired of it?" his ex had asked the last day he'd seen her.

"Tired of what?" he'd asked. He'd been hung over again. Didn't want to talk but knew from experience the fastest way to get her to shut up was to answer her questions.

"This," she'd said, waving a hand toward him. "Being hung over. Being drunk. Don't you ever crave, I don't know," she'd said, pinching the bridge of her nose between her finger and thumb. "Waking up feeling good? Clean?"

He'd laughed. When in his life had he ever felt like that?

Now he moaned, willed the cave walls to stop spinning. He tried to talk to Maria, tell her that he was going to find something to help her. But no words came out, just strange, garbled sounds.

Anger stabbed the walls of his belly. He was helpless. Useless. He scrubbed his hands over his face. His stomach pitched as he looked around. A jug of water, half-filled stood nearby. Who knew where the first aid kit was. But Clark could at least get the woman some water. He crawled to the jug, rocks biting into his palms and knees through his pants. He cursed, or tried to, when his right hand slipped off a stone and bent his wrist back.

The trip across the cave was only a few feet but it felt like miles. He was breathing hard by the time he'd dragged the jug back to Maria. He stared down at her. She was pretty. Her dark hair lay across some rumpled clothes someone had fashioned into a makeshift pillow. Her forehead was slick with sweat and a bead of it ran down her temple and into her ear. Clark looked at her neck. It was tanned and firm like the rest of her.

So easy. It would be so easy to wrap his hands around that throat and squeeze.

His hands shook at the unbidden thought. *Why would I want to do that?*

"Because you can," a voice said. Clark jerked, looked around. He could see it from the corner of his eye. He didn't want to turn the rest of the way to see all of it, but knew he would. A coldness crept over him, like when he'd stood in front of the freezer as a kid, trying to cool off on a hot summer's day. It was the same voice that he'd heard earlier, when he'd gone looking for branches. It was the shadow.

"Go ahead," the voice said again. It sounded old and wispy. Like a sigh through branches of a tree. "You'll be helping her. Ending her misery. Can't you feel it, Clark? The smoothness of her skin? Touch it and see."

Clark watched his hands drop the jug of water. It fell to its side. The dull red cap stayed in place, the water sloshed back and forth like the sea. *No, no, no.* As though watching a movie, he saw his hands moving in slow motion, toward the woman's neck. He could see his hands moving but couldn't control them, couldn't stop them. Just like when he'd cut out his tongue. There hadn't even been blood. The shadow had entered him somehow, filled his mouth with smoke and then the pain had stopped.

"Go ahead," the voice said.

He could see smoke leaking out from behind the edges of his vision. Don't look. Do not look. Instead his eyes were on her. Her skin was hot. He could feel it scalding him, heating the callouses of his hands.

"Higher," the voice encouraged. "Put your hands up higher, close to her face and squeeze."

I don't want to do it, Clark argued. This isn't me.

"Of course it is," the voice responded. Iciness bloomed near Clark's head, wrapping him in cold. He could see the tendrils of black smoke wafting into his vision now. The shadow man forming and un-forming, undulating in the dark, murky confines of the cave.

"You've wanted to do this to the fairer sex for a long time. Women have always hurt you, haven't they? Name one who has ever been there for you, been kind to you—truly kind—without wanting something from you."

Clark couldn't remember. His breath came in hitching gasps, the only sound other than water dripping. He could feel the woman's pulse under the joints of his thumbs.

"Your own mother, Clark," the voice was louder, hissing in his ears. "Your own mother. You haven't drunk away those memories, have you?" The voice was growing louder, its wispy sighs turning into a harsher sound. It filled the space and bounced off the rock walls. Then it laughed, a harsh, grating sound.

Clark ducked his head low, swiped his face over his forearm, hands still held lightly around the woman's throat. They felt glued there. Unmovable.

"Just do it, Clark," the voice encouraged, whispery once again in the firelight. "Do it and be done with this charade. You're no different than you always were. You were a bad kid and a worthless man. Embrace it. Don't hide anymore. Do you really think counseling is going to change you? You think talking about your feelings," the voice said the word with a sneer, "is going to help you become someone else?"

It might. It could.

"It won't," the voice said. Ice particles glittered on the hair on Clark's forearms. What the hell was happening?

"Just press. You'll be free then, Clark. Free to be who you really are."

Heat rose up in his chest in waves. It radiated from somewhere deep inside—his gut?—and into his chest, then through his arms. The woman moaned again, moved her head a bit to the left. Her eyelids fluttered.

Clark felt his hands tightening. He couldn't control them.

No. I don't want to do this.

"You do." The voice was louder, circling his head like a python, whispering into the parts of him that he hadn't remembered since boyhood. The weak parts. The angry parts. The parts that were dark and shoved behind walls that he'd spent years erecting.

Clark felt ice climbing down his arms, melding his hard hands onto the soft throat. As though they were one. One unit. One nation. Under God. Indivisible.

No, not indivisible. I'm not her and she isn't me. This isn't what I want. I can't—

"Finish it," the voice hissed. Clark choked out a gasp, his hands shook. The shadow man was fully formed now. He stood over Clark and the woman on the ground, his height impossibly tall, his shape lengthening and stretching.

"Give her what she deserves," the shadow man's voice barked.

Clark felt himself crumbling, down into dust, into the core of what he was. Even now after all this time, he was still the same. The voice was right.

Chapter Twenty-Five

"Run!" Dell yelled again. Addie's body, motionless, finally jerked into gear. Like a windup toy coming to life, her extremities started to move. Her feet jumped and skirted rocks, her arms pumped by her sides. A lump of fear closed her throat. She could barely breathe.

"Dell?" she called back over her shoulder. No answer. The water in the nearby stream pounded like a huge kettle drum, throbbing. Addie grappled over rocks taller than herself, slinging her body up and over. Pain registered in short bursts from various points in her body: right knee throbbing from earlier fall; left hand scraped against last boulder, right ankle twisted and sore. Shins banging into unforgiving stone.

She kept running.

Addie couldn't hear anything now except a dull roar in her head. Was it the water or her breath? Or had she stopped breathing? Everything felt light and whirly. If she could just stop for a moment …

Stars broke out across her forehead and a sharp pain

exploded on her temples. Someone had hit her. Something? The creature. A rock? Addie felt warm liquid trickling down into the collar of her jacket. The last thing she saw before she fell was a stone overhang.

She heard the voices before she opened her eyes. "Addie, get up," a familiar voice called.

Addie sighed and snuggled deeper into the blankets. Why was it so cold in here? She tried to find her pillow. It was forever falling off her bed in the night.

"Honnnnnney. We're going to be late," the voice said again. It sounded further away. Mom. Was she leaving? Addie would be late for school. Again. The last time she'd gotten detention. "Too many times tardy," the school secretary had frowned down at her. Addie had wanted to giggle and ask her to repeat the words three times fast. But she'd wisely just nodded and accepted the note requiring her to stay after school.

Addie readjusted her position. What was wrong with her bed? It felt so hard and lumpy. A smell filled the air and Addie sniffed, pulling the blankets away from her face. If Mom was still cooking breakfast then she couldn't be that late. Not yet. She stretched and sighed, sniffing the air hopefully for the smell of pancakes.

Another scent filled the air, though. Addie frowned. This wasn't right. It smelled musty and old. Like the basement at her grandparents' house. Like mildew and something else. Wet dog? Addie wrinkled her nose. A stabbing pain ran up her forehead and into her scalp.

She moaned, turned over onto her side.

"Mom?" she called.

No answer. Her lips were so dry. She wet them with her tongue and tried again. "Mom?"

She couldn't hear her mother's voice but her ears slowly filled with another sound. A dull, drone. A low buzzing. A plane? Too loud. What, then?

Addie sat up. Or tried to. The blankets were weighing her down. She shoved, pushing her hands against them. Her arms ached, her chest was tight and her head was throbbing. Addie put a hand to her head. Something tacky and warm stuck to her face. It itched. She tried to scratch it but her hand wouldn't move the right way. Panic skittered up her backbone.

She opened her eyes. Darkness. But slowly, as they adjusted, Addie could pick out lumpy shapes. This wasn't her bedroom.

The cave.

She closed her eyes again. Willed them to see something else when she opened them again. But no, it was the same both the second and third time. She moaned. Trying to sit up made her head feel like it was going to split directly down the middle. She moved a hand to her forehead. Her fingers grazed her temple, felt that same warm goo. Blood. Hers? What had happened?

"Run!" Dell had said. Dell. Where was he?

Addie looked behind her but only dim light was visible. They'd both been running from the …

A sharp inhale made her realize how sore her ribcage was.

She rubbed her side and slowly, very slowly, pushed her hands down onto the floor, used them to propel her upright. The walls of the cave and the sound of water smashing over rocks all pressed down on her. Her stomach heaved once and she retched, bringing up nothing but bile. God, her head.

Dell. She had to find him. The flashlight. Where was it? How far had she gotten before she'd fallen? Or, judging from the lump and blood on her head, until she'd run into something. She looked upward, but it was too dark to see anything other than darker, lumpier shapes.

Still on her knees, Addie patted the ground. Seconds later her fingers connected with the smooth cylinder of the flashlight. She flicked it on, shining it around the immediate area, putting a steadying hand to the wall closest to her when the dizziness got worse. There was no sign of Dell. Addie started to retrace her steps but then stopped. What if that thing was there, hiding in the shadows? She had no weapon, could barely stand upright. What would she do if it came after her?

Everything in her said to get out of there, go back to the makeshift camp and wait until morning, until Clark was more coherent or Maria could walk. Until help arrived. But none of those things were going to happen. Maybe Clark would be able to help sometime and Maria would be able to walk somewhat but neither of them were going to be able to make it down here—they both needed medical attention. Gabe was gone. Alaska was gone. Help wasn't coming. No one even knew where they were.

Addie stifled a sob. She couldn't fall apart, not now. She

rubbed her face on the sleeve of her shirt. She would look for Dell. If he was still here, still alive, she'd—*do what?*

"I'll figure it out." The words sounded small in the dark space. Slowly, using rocks and boulders as guides to place her free hand, she headed in the direction she'd come from.

Chapter Twenty-Six

Maria turned her head. It felt huge and hot—like a hot air balloon. Stupid thought. She'd like to be a balloon right now though, filled with enough helium to pull her up and into the sky. She'd float along on a breeze. Would her desire to go home be enough to bring her there?

She pictured herself, a bright red balloon on a string, floating up and over the rain. Rain. It would feel good on her hot skin. No, that wasn't right. Balloons didn't have skin. Just latex or rubber, right? Whatever it was, the rain would be refreshing.

As a girl she and her sister would press their hands against party balloons, she remembered. Turning them this way and that, making funny, squeaking sounds and laughing. She felt that way now, pressed and squeezed. Her neck. What was touching her? She struggled to open her eyelids but they felt weighted. She moaned slightly, turned her head. Was it a snake? She hated them, their quickness and dry, muscled bodies. Copper and black, or maybe green with stripes of orange. Which was the one that choked its prey?

Air. Maria turned her head to the side, trying to loosen the grip of the snake around her neck. Her hot skin felt like it would peel off under the pressure. She tried to draw a breath but her windpipe was like a crumpled drinking straw. She should fight. She should move. But she could only moan. Pressure built behind her eyelids. Would they pop out of her skull? Air. Please, just a little.

A grating sound filled the air. The firelight flickering behind her closed lids started to fade. Maria started to thrash, every cell in her body fighting for air. But she was so weak. Liquid limbs. She turned her head again, toward the pressure, toward the snake. Tried to form a word but it died on her lips. Maria tried to open her eyes. Blackness started to seep in.

And then, suddenly, the pressure was gone. She gulped in great breaths of air. The sound was ragged in her ears. For a moment the strange, grating sound was deafening. It filled the cave completely. She wanted to clamp her hands over her ears.

Then, suddenly, all the noise faded away. Maria lay on the sleeping bag breathing. Just breathing. Luxuriating in the simple, unconscious act; filling her lungs with sweet, pure air. She continued breathing, turned her head and slowly, with much effort, opened her eyes.

A face lay just inches from her own. A man's face, grimacing in pain. Her breath became shallower, her eyes widened. Slowly, her gaze moved from the awful clenched face to the man's torso. Between his calloused hands was a long, thin blade. A knife. No, it was dark and jagged. A stone. Shale, maybe. Pointed and sharp. The man's hands wrapped around it dripped with blood. More blood pulsed from the spot in his chest where the rock had been stabbed in.

Maria tried to scream but the only sound that came to her lips was a dull, dry moan. Her eyes were too dry to form tears.

It was Clark. And he was dead.

Addie picked her way carefully across the floor of the cave. Her hand felt damp on the flashlight, her eyes adjusting to the dimness of the cave enough that she flicked it off, using it just when the shadows made it impossible to see where she was going. These were the only batteries she had. Climbing back up the ravine and finding her way to camp in the dark wasn't something she wanted to do. She'd make these last.

Her head throbbed, a steady staccato beat. What were the signs of concussion? She tried to remember from the boys' early years playing sports but couldn't. How stupid could she be, running into a rock wall? While Dell sacrificed himself for her. No, not sacrificed. There was no proof that he'd been hurt or—she shivered—anything worse.

The brook on her left branched off, away from the cave at last, flowing into some sort of underground tunnel. Slowly, the noise became more muted. How far back did this cave go? The longest cave in the world extended more than 300 miles, Mammoth Cave in Kentucky. Or was it Tennessee? No, Kentucky. She'd read it in a *National Geographic* or a *Smithsonian* magazine once. Or had one of the boys told her? Why could she remember that bit of trivia but not more about concussions?

The boys. Addie stopped for a moment, closed her eyes. Images of her sons sitting on the couch near her, tossing popcorn into their mouths and laughing at whatever was on the screen.

Don't think it. Don't.

Bright curtains framing an autumn scene outside the window, the sound of birds, the smell of the coffee: dry and slightly acidic.

A sound snapped her reverie. Scratching. Claws? She held her breath, listened hard. The only sound other than the dull pulse of the water was her heartbeat loud in her ears. Addie exhaled slowly, turned the flashlight back on. Walking forward, as quickly as she could over the stones and rocks, she crisscrossed the floor of the cave. The sound came again.

It was coming from higher up than where she stood. She started climbing in that direction. Her hands were damp and so was her shirt, the material bunching around her elbows where she'd pushed it up. She tugged the sleeves down now.

Another sound. What was it? A sort of scuttling sound or of something metallic skimming across something hard and nonresistant. A dull yellow light gleamed from up higher. Addie sped up, skinned her shin on the face of a stone and held in a cry of pain. She wanted to stop to rub the area but didn't. Instead she used the pale light ahead of her to guide her. More rocks, more stones to maneuver.

Then she was there, outside of what appeared to be a room in the cave. The entrance to it was rounded, like the archways in mid-century houses. Addie put a hand to the surface to steady herself. The rock under her hand was smooth, satin-like and ice cold. The light ahead of her, in the space, flickered. Addie squatted, her body pressed into the outside wall and peered into the interior. Whatever was in there, she didn't want it to see her.

The grating sound filled the air, louder and closer. It wasn't coming from this room though, but from behind Addie. Her breath caught in her chest. She could see something in the space, a dark shape. Tall, stooped as though it was crouching, too. She couldn't see the ceiling of this room. Her eyes skimmed the rest of the area. If only she could flick on the flashlight and see more clearly.

A moan filled the space. Dell. She leaned forward, not bothering anymore to keep her body hidden behind the archway. She had to see …

The shape inside the room straightened slightly, held its head forward, cocking it in her direction. It sniffed the air. Breath whooshed through its nostrils. The shape turned, its body taking up more space as it looked headlong into the entryway where Addie crouched. Still as a pillar, she stood. Her pulse jumped in her neck and wrists.

Another moan from somewhere to the side of the room. Addie let out a breath in tiny increments between her teeth as the shape moved in that direction. Its legs were bowed, it's body, she could see in the dim light, covered in thick, matted hair. It looked exactly like an ape, though larger, much larger. As it looked past her out toward the sound, her arms trembled and jumped over her mid-section. She held her tongue between her teeth until she tasted blood.

Addie felt her way against the wall. Don't trip. Do not trip, she told herself with every step. Pressing her lips together, she silenced her breath and the sound of her teeth chattering.

"Uggghmmm," a voice said. It was male. Dell. Addie's ribcage rose and fell faster. He was alive. He was …

The creature bent toward him. The grating sound was getting louder. The creature heard it too, swung its big head from one side to the other as though trying to locate the source of the noise. Then it shook its head, like a bear.

She looked over her shoulder, trying to see where the sounds were coming from, then back to Dell. The Bigfoot bent nearer to Dell's prone body and lifted it. Cradled in the massive furry arms, the doctor looked like a baby doll, small and limp.

Addie gaped. What was it doing? Surely if it had wanted to hurt him or kill him it would have done it already. And the way the creature held him, like he was fragile china or delicate glass, it was impossible. Wasn't it?

Chapter Twenty-Seven

The creature continued to move toward the back of the cave's room, holding Dell. Addie followed, using the wall as a guide. The light, she realized, came from beyond the room itself. Curious, she watched it flicker as she moved. A fire? Would that thing know how to make one? And what was it going to do with Dell?

The scratching, grating sound grew louder, closer. The creature moved more quickly and looked over its shoulder again and again. It didn't make any noise, except for the small huffing sounds its breath made. Addie struggled to keep up but couldn't. Her legs ached, her back and arms felt like rubber. She paused for a second, swiped hair out of her eyes and then pressed on. She was so close. If Dell were in her place, surely he would try to save her. The creature glided effortlessly out of the room and into the place where the light was. She was being left behind. She was too slow, too tired.

Addie felt the hair on the back of her neck stand on end and the skin along her backbone quivered. What was that noise? She turned, again searching for movement behind her but saw nothing but darkness. Another sound joined the first sounds though, a weird sort of whispering moan. She shoved her way forward, stumbled and caught herself then entered the room beyond.

The creature stood against the far wall of another room. Dell was just as limp in its arms, his head hanging to one side, his glasses crooked. The Bigfoot turned as Addie stepped into the space. The light was yellow and flickered from what looked like an old oil lantern by the side wall.

The temperature fell suddenly by twenty degrees, the hair on her arms standing on end. She looked again behind her. In the shadows of the cave walls there stood a shadowy figure. Like a man. Or was it smoke? She squinted. Was it real or her imagination? The shadow man glided closer. He too, was tall, though his form grew and shrank and undulated like he was made of water.

The air continued to get colder. Addie could see her breath now. The shadow-thing seemed to bring the cold with it, darkness rolled off the figure like a vapor. It was a figure now, though, easier to make out the shape of legs and arms and head. Behind her, Addie heard the creature, the Bigfoot, make a noise. She turned back around and it opened its mouth. Its teeth were yellowed and square, spaces between almost big enough for Addie's fingers to fit in easily. A sound came from its mouth, like a train and it roared through the space. Deafening. Addie yelped and covered her ears with both hands, bringing her elbows to her knees.

Then, just as quickly as it had come, the growl died away. Addie looked up again. The creature was looking toward the doorway she stood just inside of. Its big head swung toward the rear of the space. There was another opening there, like a door. She nearly laughed, hysteria bubbling between her ribs. Was it trying to tell her to follow it? Dell moaned in the creature's arms, one leg jerking in a spasm. The creature adjusted its grip and moved its head again, looking at Addie. Its eyes were so gold they looked fluid.

She stood, unmoving. The shadow man was making the moaning sound again and she turned to look, then glanced back to see the creature gliding from the room, Dell in its arms.

"Wait!" she called out. "Wait for me. Don't hurt him."

She scrambled over rocks feeling the coldness of the space seep into her bones and tendons. Grabbing the lantern, she ran, stumbled, tripped, after the Bigfoot.

But it was gone. The blackness behind her, cold and menacing, pressed against her legs and torso.

Maria slowly, slowly changed her position. Her head felt full of cotton batting, like a pillow or an extra-thick quilt was stuffed inside of her skull. Her left leg felt like a giant toothache, pulsing with every beat of her heart. She moaned as she carefully turned to her side and pushed herself to a seated position. The cave walls swirled and she put a hand to her mouth. She sat with her eyes closed for several minutes, listening to the ragged sound of her breath and the far-off tumble of water over stone. Outside, the rain had stopped. After several deep breaths, Maria opened her eyes and looked to the entrance of the cave. Rainwater still dripped off nearby tree leaves and onto the ground below.

What time was it? The moon was still hidden by thick clouds. She'd been sleeping but for how long? Hours? Days? Nausea grew and crested in her belly, like a wave in the sea. She breathed in and out, concentrated only on the pull and push of breath. Gently, she changed position. Careful to avoid looking at the man on the floor nearby, Maria moved into a one-legged crouch. Fire shot up her injured leg, despite her attempt to shield it from any pressure. She gasped and fell to her side, the pain shocking her into losing her balance.

Tears welled up in her eyes and she closed them again. Maybe it was better to just play dead. Maybe it would be better to just be dead. Tears leaked through her eyelids and ran down her cheeks. She was so tired.

No. She had to get up. Get moving. Try to find help. Who had done this to Clark? Gabe. He'd come back and murdered Clark while she was sleeping. Was it Gabe who'd tried to strangle her? She had to get away before he came back for her.

Where were the others? Maria opened her eyes and looked around. She'd assumed they were sleeping nearby but the space was empty except for miscellaneous pieces of clothes. Alone. She was utterly, completely alone.

There was a sound outdoors, the rustling of branches. Then a snap as one broke. Maria looked around her again, wildly. Gabe. She turned on her side, shook Clark.

Stupid. He's dead. Dead! His hands and arms bounced lightly under the pressure. The one holding the rock-knife slid down to the ground, releasing the makeshift blade. Maria stared at it. Blood had started to gum its surface and pools of it ran from his hand when it touched the earth. Suddenly she understood. He'd stabbed himself. But why? Had Gabe made him?

Maria didn't have time to think any longer about it because more branches broke outside, then the clear sound of footsteps drawing closer. She moved quickly, too quickly to think about what she was doing. She grabbed the dead man's hand, covering her own in his blood then smeared it over her chest and neck. She dipped her hand down again and once more, gagging as the smell hit her nose.

Then, before she could vomit, she snatched the makeshift blade from his hand and pressed it into her own, tucked her hand under her blanket and waited. If Gabe didn't look closely, didn't check for pulses, he would assume they were both dead. If he did bother to check, Maria would have to kill him. Or try.

Her fingers tightened over the stone, the sharp edges digging into her flesh.

Chapter Twenty-Eight

The scuttling sound grew louder. Addie ran faster. She launched herself over medium sized rocks, slid on smaller ones and nearly tripped as she rounded a bend in the tunnel. With the sound behind her came extreme cold.

The lantern beam bounced through the tunnel, the walls getting more and more narrow. Addie heard a loud click and then a whir behind her and then heard a voice. It sounded wispy at first, she had to strain to hear it over her gasping breath.

"Don't run," it said. "You're so tired. Just sit and rest a bit. You'll never catch up now."

She looked over her shoulder without slowing her stride. She swung her head around just in time to avoid colliding into a wall. As she bounced the light over its surface, she saw an opening up high. It was wide and from it came a strange bluish light. Like a turret window. Too high to reach, the opening must have been nine feet from the floor of the cave.

"Help!" she cried. "Someone help me!"

The voice behind her got louder.

"Why are you bothering?" The voice slithered into her ears, slimy like an eel. "Aren't you tired? You can rest, Addie. Just stop and come to me. I'll help you."

Now the voice turned soft, gentle. For a moment Addie stood, one foot on a rock, the other trying desperately to find a toe hole on the wall in front of her. Trying to launch herself somehow into the space above her.

What was the use? She was exhausted. Lost. Cold. Every muscle in her body hurt, every tendon and ligament. Even if she could eventually catch up with Dell, how would she get him away from that creature?

The voice spoke again, caressing the air around her with sweet words. The scratching sound was soft now, muted. Like a gentle tapping.

"Let me help you rest. Come with me now, it will feel so good to just let go, won't it?"

Yes. It would feel so good. Just to rest, to think. Maybe just for a minute …

"That's right, just for a minute or two. He wouldn't have followed you this far, you know. You've already gone above and beyond what is expected from you," the voice said, growing lower and quieter.

"The good doctor is selfish," the voice continued. Addie couldn't explain it but it felt as though the voice itself was caressing her, molding itself around her like a blanket. She looked from the opening up high to see the shadow man was standing very near to her.

"Selfish and only concerned with his own genius, his own agenda," the voice murmured. "Why else would he have stranded you here? Defenseless and alone. All alone." The last word was drawn out in conjunction with a deep sigh. Addie felt a sigh of her own pass through her lips. The foot that was propped on the wall, searching for a spot to climb upward, dropped to the cave floor.

The shadow was made of black vapor. She could see it in the dim lantern light, the edges of his outline dissipating in the air around her. And then a wisp of the black smoke touched her calf. Through her pants she could feel the iciness.

It was true, though wasn't it? Dell was only concerned with himself, his practice and patients. Why had he even asked her on this trip anyway? To impress her and their motley little band of anxiety-ridden clients with his outdoor prowess. Heat bubbled in Addie's chest and it felt good, warming. It was strange too though, unexpected. It took a moment for her to realize what the emotion was. Anger. Rage, really. It made sense though, didn't it? Why shouldn't she feel angry at him? She may never make it home safely again, never see her boys, never …

The voice was saying something. Addie shook her head, tried to clear away the cobwebs. Why did everything in her brain suddenly seem to be moving so slowly? Her thoughts felt thick, sticky, like days-old coffee, sludge trapped between the two hemispheres. The wisps of blackness were covering her arms now, and maybe her neck. She felt weak.

"… doesn't it? You need to think of yourself, not him. He used you, just like all men do. Just like your ex-husband. Used what he wanted and left you to pick up all the pieces.

Take care of your two boys. And then there was your father," the voice made the same sighing sound, as though it was sad, so sad to remind Addie of these facts. "He never cared for you, did he? Deserted you, left you and your mother without a backward glance."

It struck her suddenly, through the pea soup that had once been her brain that this voice, this thing, knew so much about her. How could that be?

"Never mind," the voice said, though she was sure she hadn't spoken the words out loud. Had she?

"It doesn't matter how I know, just that I can help you." The voice was butter, warm and silky now. "You want help, don't you? Want to get out of this place, be free?" It sighed again, slithering into the corners of the room.

"Come with me," it said. "I can help you."

Addie nodded dumbly and turned away from the wall, away from the strange blue glow on the other side of the opening. Yes, this was right. She should go with this voice. It cared for her. It would help her.

She put a hand out in front of her, trying to see into the thick blackness. But there was nothing. Just icy coldness and then the grating sound once again filling the space. It was louder now. Louder and louder and Addie wanted to put her hands over her ears but when she tried, she realized they were already there, clamped over either side of her head.

Then another sound split the air and Addie doubled over, the pain in her head magnified as the sound of a train roared through the space. She smelled the familiar musty smell, like wet dog and pond scum and then she felt something warm and thick pulling her to her feet. She opened her eyes, looked wildly around as the creature, the same creature that had carried Dell off, grabbed her in its grip and hauled her upward.

Addie tried to move, to think, to do something. But she could only stare, eyes wide, as the creature pressed her to its chest and grunting, hauled her upward to the opening where the light came from.

Behind her, Addie heard the grating grow louder. Then the voice, the same one that had been speaking to her so gently and reassuringly, yelled, "No!" into the darkness.

Chapter Twenty-Nine

The footsteps drew closer. Maria forced her eyelids to relax, rolling her eyes back in her head so that they wouldn't flutter open unconsciously.

Step. Step. Step. A voice cursed. One that was familiar to her but strangely out of place. How could it be? Maria's eyelids flew open and she jerked upward.

A tall figure stood nearby, hands on hips. The hair was no longer shiny and swingy, but tangled, dusted with bits of dried leaves and twigs.

"You're alive?" Alaska gasped. She rushed toward Maria but stopped abruptly over Clark's body. "What happened? Is he ..."

Maria started to speak, but her words knotted into each until she was stuttering, then sobbing. Alaska sank down beside her, patting Maria's shoulders awkwardly. Maria should feel embarrassed about the wrenching, gulping sobs. Should be embarrassed to let a stranger see her this way. But all that she felt was a deep, profound relief.

Finally, long minutes later, the sobs ran out. Maria sat taking shuddering breaths.

"What the hell happened?" Alaska asked.

"What happened to you? We thought you were dead."

"No. I'm fine. Just got misplaced. I fell, lost my pack somewhere along the way. I thought …" Alaska paused. "Where are the others? It feels like weeks since I've talked to someone."

Maria adjusted her position and winced, pain radiating up her leg. "They're; I'm not sure where everyone else is."

"Are you hurt?"

She nodded in response. "My leg. Gabe. Have you seen him?"

"Seen Gabe?" Alaska asked, surprised. "No. Hasn't he been here with the group?"

"There is no group. Clark," Maria's eyes automatically went to the man prone beside her on the rocky floor. "I'm not sure what happened. I was unconscious for a while. The pain was too much." She paused, bit her lip. "My leg is broken. I was trying to get away, to get away from him. I don't know where the others are. Gabe …" her voice drifted off for a moment.

The words tumbled out then, over and over she interrupted her own thought process, began sentences and then left others hanging unfinished. She told about what had happened since they arrived at the cave: Dr. O'Dell suffering hypothermia, Clark losing his tongue, Gabe attacking her, the box of old papers they'd found describing other strange and bad things happening here. The monster with the golden eyes and the shadow thing that she'd seen hovering near Gabe by the fire.

"How can any of this be happening?" Alaska asked after Maria had run out of words. "I just ... man, I thought I had it bad."

"What did happen to you?" Maria asked. "And can I please have some water." She moved again, slightly, and winced.

"Of course," Alaska pawed through the miscellaneous items strewn over the floor of the cave, then brought Maria a jug partially filled with water. She helped her to lean back enough to drink.

"Let me look at your leg while I tell you what happened to me. Don't worry," she said with a smile as Maria started to protest, "I got my first aid badge in Girl Scouts."

Alaska moved the jug of water out of the way, and then slowly, unbandaged the leg. She mumbled something Maria couldn't make out as she searched through the strewn clothing in the area, bending over Clark at one point and removing his belt. Maria turned away as she did. She should ask if the other woman needed help, but couldn't. She closed her eyes instead and wished for a big bottle of painkillers.

Alaska bent over Maria's leg, undoing the work of Dr. O'Dell and restarting the splint from scratch. Her hands were cool on the hot, swollen skin of Maria's leg. While she worked, Alaska started to talk.

"I got lost trying to find the cave. I can't read a topographical map to save my life but David, uh, Dr. O'Dell didn't know that. It was only ten minutes from the trail and I have a good sense of direction. I thought I'd just find it." She paused, starting a tear in a long-sleeved shirt with her teeth and ripping it into a long, thin strip.

"Then I fell down a ravine and lost my pack in the process. That was the second jackass move on my part. I blacked out, not for long I don't think. When I came to, I was disoriented. I backtracked the way I'd come. At least I thought I did. But I ended up going around in circles. It was starting to rain and I felt dizzy. I just stood under a tree for a while, trying to figure out what to do next."

Alaska frowned at Maria. "This next part might be a little uncomfortable."

Maria nodded, swallowed. Her leg was bloated, crisscrossed with red where the bandages had been tied tightly. She couldn't see a bone protruding but looked away before she did. How was she going to get out of the woods? The pain had felt like a dull toothache before, but now was sharp and pointed. Alaska's hands were confident but gentle. Carefully she wrapped the fresh bandages.

"Just try to relax," Alaska said as she wound them around and over Maria's leg. "Where was I in my story?"

Maria knew the other woman was trying to distract her from the pain radiating up her leg. She felt grateful rather than annoyed at that.

"It was just starting to rain," Maria said through clenched teeth.

"That's right," Alaska said. "It turned into a torrential downpour and I gave up hope of following any of my tracks back. It hadn't worked very well when I could see clearly. In the mud, I knew it was useless. So I decided to find shelter and wait out the storm."

"Only it didn't stop until now."

Alaska nodded. "Well, it took me a while to find you, to find this cave."

She finished with Maria's leg and sat back on her haunches, staring into the dwindling fire.

"So, what do we do now?" she asked.

Addie's eyes flew open. The sound of ragged breath filled her ears and she realized it was coming from her own mouth. Looking wildly around the area, she saw Dell lying nearby. The creature was nowhere to be seen.

"Dell?" She moved closer, shook the man's shoulders. He jerked upright, arms and legs flailing for an instant before she put a reassuring arm on his shoulder.

"It's me, Addie. Adeline. Are you alright?"

"What …? What happened? Where are we?" His voice was thick. He sounded sleepy.

"We're … well, I'm not sure. Somewhere in the cave, way in a tunnel or room or something. Far to the back. The creature …" This time it was Addie's voice that trailed off. Had she really seen what she thought she had? Was it possible?

The sound of the grating, scratching and the low, gentle whisper filled her memory. She shivered in response.

"I think it saved us."

Dell stared at Addie.

"What?"

"I know it sounds crazy, but I think it saved us from something else. Something worse. What do you remember before you lost consciousness?"

Dell frowned, then closed his eyes. For a minute, Addie

worried that he was gone again, but his brow wrinkled and then he opened his eyes.

"We were running, trying to get out of the ravine. You were ahead of me and I told you to run because we'd just seen … something. And I saw you ahead of me, with the light. And then I heard the noises behind me and I knew I wasn't going to make it."

"That's right," Addie said, her voice rising in excitement. "What noises did you hear though, do you remember?"

Dell moved a hand heavily to his face, rubbed it for several long seconds.

"Like nails over a chalkboard," he said finally.

"Right," Addie nodded. "But that's not the sound the creature makes. I heard that sound earlier, in the cave too, and then right before we ended up here. I think I heard it earlier even, up in the cave entrance, but it doesn't matter now. There is something else here, something bad in the cave and I think that that … that thing—the creature, Bigfoot, whatever it is—is protecting us from it."

Addie's voice was climbing higher and she took a deep breath before continuing.

"Remember the drawings in the cave's entrance?"

Dell nodded, eyes closing again.

"I think they have something to do with the other thing, the shadow thing that makes the strange noises. I know it sounds crazy," Addie rushed on, her breath coming faster. "But I think in some way that the creature is keeping us safe from that. Whatever that is. Maybe a spirit or an entity of some kind. You said yourself that caves are often thought of as spiritual places, right?"

Dell nodded then opened his eyes and looked at her. Behind the cracked lens one of his eyes looked smaller and darker.

"So your premise is what, Adeline? That an evil spirit is roaming this cave?"

His voice was low but it held the faint incredulity of a professional being told a ghost story by a kid at summer camp. And suddenly, that was exactly how Addie felt.

Addie forced her voice to remain calm. "No. At least, I can't prove any of it. I just—"

"I'm sorry, Adeline," Dell interrupted. "We don't have time for this right now. Whatever that thing is—a mutant, a psychopath dressed in a gorilla costume—we've got to get out of here. Back to the others. Can you walk?"

Addie wanted to scream. It was *a creature* and that wasn't what she was worried about. She was worried about the other thing, the shadow man that spoke so gently and made her insides turn to mush. The thing that knew so much about her. She sat for a moment, energy leaking out of her like a balloon losing air. Dell was right, she knew that. There would be time later to discuss this. But how could he not believe her? He'd seen part of it—the creature—with his own eyes, hadn't he?

"I can walk," she said finally. "Can you?"

Dell grimaced and slowly started to get to his feet. Addie jumped up, muscles aching and sore, scrapes on her shins hot and throbbing. She wormed her way under his arm, helped prop him to his feet. He stood there, slowly for a few seconds, taking in a big, deep breath. Then he removed his arm and touched his fingers lightly to the wall nearest him.

"I'm all right," he said. "As long as we go slowly, I'll be fine."

"What about that," Addie asked, jerking her head to the lantern nearby. "Should we take it with us?"

Dell nodded and Addie left his side. The lantern was old, Addie had been right. It burned oil and looked heavy. She stood for a few seconds, mesmerized by the flame that glowed and shook behind the glass.

Chapter Thirty

Maria stared at Alaska, her eyes wide. She was a beautiful young woman, something innocent and pure about her. In her real life, Alaska would have hated her, seen her automatically as competition in her personal life or an inept weight on her shoulders at work. But here ... here things were different. She felt, oddly, protective of the younger woman. The feeling was unfamiliar, strange. Uncomfortable.

Alaska stood up suddenly, her legs feeling jittery, her gut uneasy. These weird emotions, all this drama. She needed to move.

"We need to make a plan," she said. "We've got to find the others and find some food." She wanted to say, but didn't, that they needed to find Gabe, regroup. She believed Maria about the creature, about losing consciousness and not knowing what had happened to Clark. But Gabe trying to kill her? That was too unbelievable. Gabe was a gentle soul. There was no way ...

"I'm not sure how far I can make it," Maria said. "But please, please, don't leave me here alone. With him," she glanced at the dead man.

Alaska followed her gaze. He looked peaceful somehow, the lines and hardness of his face gentle and softer now. As though the tight anger and rage that had simmered just under his surface had seeped out of him like the blood pooled under his back. Alaska remembered seeing the faces of many other dead, the horror at first when she'd been old enough to visit her family's funeral home, then the acceptance and later, the indifference. Dead bodies were just shells.

When she was a kid her brother had kept hermit crabs as pets. She'd been fascinated when it was time for the creatures to shed their old, too-small shells and find new homes in roomier ones. The dead reminded her of that. Shells left while the spirit sought a bigger, freer space.

"Let's get you up and see what you've got," Alaska said, stooping to swing the other woman's arm across her shoulders.

"Ready?" she asked.

Maria shook her head. "Not really."

"Just try," Alaska said, and pulled.

Dell could hear Adeline behind him, infrequent grunts or sighs as she stumbled on the uneven cave floor. It had been a challenge to climb down from the odd room-like part of the cave, a time-consuming process that had left him weak limbed. He felt helpless and frustrated. He wished he could pull up the emotion of anger. It would be a welcome relief.

He thought of Clark. Now there was a man with plenty of anger to go around. But thoughts of his client brought up an image of the last time he'd seen him. The man's missing tongue. How …?

No. Dell gave himself a mental shake, hard enough to dislodge the thought. He wasn't in a place to analyze now, to figure things out. None of this trip was making sense. Nothing had gone the way he'd planned. None of what he'd expected to happen had and things he couldn't have imagined just yesterday had formed a sort of horror movie in his mind.

"… have any?" Adeline's voice broke into his thoughts.

"What?" He paused, turned behind him. She stumbled on another rock, and he put out a hand automatically to catch her. Her head was low and she didn't see his outstretched hand until her shoulder bumped into it. She jumped, startled.

"Sorry," he said. "I couldn't hear you." The sound of the water in the underground brook was becoming louder. A good sign. They must be getting closer to camp.

"I just asked if you had any water left. I think I lost my bottle somewhere."

Dell pulled off his pack, lowered it to the ground and found the dented bottle in a side pocket. He passed it to Adeline. She smiled, and tipped the bottle up, took two small swigs.

"Have more," he said. "There's plenty at camp. I think we're getting close."

She smiled again, and took several larger swallows, then passed the bottle back to him.

"Thanks," she said. He nodded, took a few swigs himself

then put the water back and re-shouldered his pack. The motion nearly took him off his feet.

"You OK?" Adeline asked.

He nodded. "Fine. Let's keep going." He smiled at her, tried to take the stiffness out of his voice. It wasn't her fault they were here. Outdoorsman. The word brought a twisted smile to his face. His legs were weak, his head ached.

They walked on. The uneven, rocky surface of the cave floor made walking slow and tedious. His feet felt bruised even through his boots. It was hard to see what was in front of him too, the light from the flashlight weak against the thick darkness, the spidery crack in his glasses making half of his vision appear fragmented, disjointed.

Dell flashed the light along the cave walls every few minutes. Adeline didn't say anything but if she'd asked he would have said he was checking for bats. It wasn't true though. He was really looking for that thing, the creature that had carried him off. He didn't tell Adeline, but he remembered it scooping him up, remembered the feel of being carried, weightless in the matted, smelly arms. But was it carrying him to safety as she claimed, or back to its lair to kill him? A shiver wracked his body suddenly.

Finally, what felt like hours later, he saw light. It wasn't the light of a flashlight. Instead it danced and bounced, was bright and merry. An odd sight after the hours of pressing darkness.

"We're here," he said, his voice grateful.

"Thank God," Adeline said.

Dell pressed on, his footsteps a bit faster. He remembered

riding horses as a kid and how his pony always knew when she was getting closer to the barn, picking up her pace even after a long ride. He felt like that now. Anxious to get to the relative safety of the fire, to be with others in the group, make sure that Maria and Clark were all right.

He could see the fire now. The flames flickered and danced in the open space, illuminating a body sleeping nearby. The rest of the space, strangely, was empty. The bedding Maria had been lying on was gone as was most of the miscellaneous clothing that had been strewn on the cave's floor. He glanced up at the strange markings on the ceiling, the firelight making the white marks appear to glow. No more water dripped from the ceiling.

"Clark?" He called softly, not wanting to disturb the sleeping man but at the same time anxious to be sure he was aware of their presence.

No answer.

He tried again, a little louder. He could hear Adeline behind him. He moved closer to the sleeping man. And then he saw the blood. It formed jelly-like pools beneath his back, his chest open with a gaping, jagged wound near his heart. The material of his flannel shirt was frayed and matted with drying blood.

Adeline cried out.

Dell tried to turn, to comfort her. Instead he fell to his knees shakiness taking over his limbs.

"What happened to him?" Addie's voice sounded unnatural. Wooden and stiff like a board. Stiff as a board. Wasn't that a term used to describe the dead? She held back a laugh.

Hysteria. That's all it is, a calm voice rationalized in her head. But the other half of her nearly guffawed in response. She couldn't quite merge the events of the past two days together in her head: the storm, the cave with its strange symbols and smells and sounds, the creature and the shadow man. Maria hurt, now gone, along with Gabe and Alaska. And now this. Her gaze returned to the prone body near the fire. He looked peaceful at least, as though some of the rage that had coursed through him, the meanness, had leaked out like air from a balloon.

"Where could Maria be?" her voice wobbled like a top.

"She was injured. She couldn't have gone far," Dell said. His eyes were trained on the body of his client, his voice too, sounded unsteady.

Which one of them would fall apart first?

"Unless…" she let go of the rest of her sentence and it floated out into the darkness.

Dell looked at her.

"Unless the creature came and carried her away?" Dell asked, his voice laced with sarcasm. "Or maybe the dark shadow spirit?"

A press of white-hot anger singed Addie's stomach.

"Look, you heard and saw what I did back there," she said, the words acidic in her throat "How do you explain it?"

"Not through dark fairy tales and horror movie plots," Dell shot back. He rubbed a hand over the back of his neck.

They stood in angry silence for a few minutes, both looking anywhere but at each other. Addie crossed her arms.

Every bit of skin was bruised, scratched or icy cold.

"Sorry," he mumbled finally. "I'm not in the best frame of mind right now."

Addie said nothing, just nodded, trying to avert her eyes from the dead man. It was like a car wreck though, her eyes just kept returning.

"We need to go and look for her," she said finally able to tear her gaze away. "She's injured and needs our help. And we should cover," her voice stumbled, "him with something."

Dell didn't respond, just nodded. He looked old and gray in the pale light. His face was lined and the shadows from the firelight cast his eyes in dark recesses, making the sockets look hollow. Addie straightened her shoulders, pushed out a big breath. What she wanted was nothing more than to crawl into a sleeping bag, preferably far away from this cave, and sleep for weeks. She glanced toward the entrance of the cave. But Maria was out there somewhere. And Gabe was missing too. Had he gone for help? Tried to bring Maria along to get her the medical attention she needed? Had they thought that Addie and Dell were a lost cause, that they weren't coming back?

"We should refill your water and try to find the extra flashlight," she said, beginning to look around the makeshift campsite. "Can you get that Mylar blanket for Clark?" Her voice sounded so normal that it surprised her. She didn't feel normal. Not at all.

Minutes later Clark was covered. They had found an extra flashlight and filled a bottle three-quarters full of water from the collapsible jug. They made their way to the entrance of the cave. Dell had added some extra branches to the fire, not wanting to risk it going out while they were gone. A sudden slap of guilt hit Addie as she glanced back. It wasn't right to leave Clark like this. But Maria needed her. She sighed, body longing to slide down the side of the cave and into a puddle on the floor.

A scream, long and pain-filled, suddenly cut through the relative quiet of the night. Addie gasped. Dell ran toward the sound and Addie stumbled after him.

Chapter Thirty-One

The woods were dark, the leaves on the trees and ground drenched. Dell's right foot slipped but he righted himself, kept running toward where he thought the scream had come from. He could hear Adeline behind him, her breath ragged. She must be just as tired as he was, though she hadn't complained. A momentary twinge of guilt pinched his gut when he thought of what he'd said about the creature, the dark spirit haunting the cave. Or rather, the tone he'd used when saying it.

Another sound cut through the darkness, this time more of a moan. It came from his right and he veered in that direction. The dull tunnel of light from the flashlight bouncing erratically as he ran. He dodged a tree only to get tangled in a hanging vine. Though he'd felt damp for hours, the vine drenched him, coating his clothes and skin in a new layer of cold wetness. Shoving his way through with an angry grunt, he burst out into a small clearing.

A body lay prone on the ground, another figure standing over it. Maria, he assumed was lying there, defenseless.

"Get away from her!" his voice was loud and authoritative. The standing figure took a step back. Dell rushed forward, wishing that he had the gun he'd packed. The gun that had gone missing before they'd made camp that first day. The figure on the ground moaned again.

"Addie?" it called weakly.

Adeline rushed from behind him before he could think or grab her arm, prevent her.

"I'm here," she said, moving quickly toward the woman. "Maria, I'm here."

The other figure stood dumbly. He was tall, Dell could see, lanky. He moved toward him, holding the flashlight so that it blinded Dell.

"Don't move," Dell said, holding up a hand to shield his eyes.

"David? Dr. O'Dell. It's me."

Not a man's voice, but a woman's. Alaska? She pointed the light toward the ground and he shone his toward her, but the beam wasn't strong enough to reach. He moved closer. Finally, he could see her.

"My God," he breathed, rushing toward her. "We thought you were … how did you get here?"

Alaska Baines had been his client for months and Dell had seen many expressions on her face: anger and sadness during the grieving process, confidence, flickers of unease when he'd asked her about things she didn't want to talk about. Even, and he doubted she realized he knew this, expressions that showed hunger for him. But he'd never seen this look on her face. She looked like a child: frightened, unsure. Her hair was tangled and knotted, her legs still in the short shorts she'd been wearing when they started the trip were scraped and bruised, fresh blood coming from one shin. She looked cold and wet and miserable.

"We thought you weren't coming back, you and Dr. Preston. So we were going to try to find the trail again, try to get out of this place." Even her voice sounded different, quieter and less confident than usual. Smaller somehow. "But we didn't get far. Maria's leg is pretty bad. I re-did the brace but we'll need to make a crutch or a cane to help her balance."

"She's losing consciousness, Dell," Addie's voice broke in. "We should get her back to camp, off the wet ground."

Dell nodded, looked from Adeline back to Alaska.

"Where is Gabe?" Alaska asked.

Dell shook his head. "I don't know. We haven't seen him since earlier today. Maria said ..." his voice drifted off.

Alaska nodded. "I know, she told me. You don't believe that, do you?" Alaska had lowered her voice.

Dell shrugged. He didn't know what he believed anymore.

"Dell?"

He glanced toward Adeline who was squatting beside Maria. The young woman was pale in the beam of his flashlight, face clenched in a grimace of pain.

"Yes, of course. Let's get back to camp."

It took several long minutes for the makeshift parade to travel back to the cave. Dell and Adeline supported Maria between them and even in unconsciousness she still groaned and grimaced in pain. They'd created a makeshift chair between them, supporting the woman's legs while keeping her arms around their shoulders. Alaska shone the light and alternately readjusted Maria's arms, which kept sliding from Dell and Adeline's shoulders.

Dell's arms were shaking by the time the cave came into sight and he sighed, gratefully, when they'd deposited Maria back onto a new makeshift bed. He was tired. More tired than he could have ever imagined. The others must feel the same. He had so many questions for Alaska and so many preparations to make for the morning. His throat was dry— he needed fluids. Dell thought of all these things as he sat near the fire, feeding it branches before his body slumped, fatigue finally taking over.

He woke with a start, heart hammering. Had he been asleep hours or minutes? He glanced around him, the forms of Alaska and Adeline lying on either side of Maria. The fire was getting low. An hour then at least. Though the branches they had to keep the fire going were small and thin, so maybe not quite as long as that.

What had woken him? A sound. Rustling. Had it come from inside the cave or out? He should wake Adeline, ask her if she'd heard anything. It was a cruel thought, though. They were all exhausted; adrenaline having turned to excessive fatigue. The human body can only endure so much before …

There! The sound of rustling in the woods near the cave's

mouth again. Dell groped the ground, hand searching for a flashlight while he kept an eye on the entrance. The sky was beginning to lighten, just a little, the promise of dawn. Through the wide cave entrance, Dell saw tree branches moving. He remembered Addie's words, about the creature, the dark spirit.

Ghost stories. An overactive imagination.

Heart pounding, Dell rose to a half crouch. His right boot hit a stone and it clinked against another. To him it sounded like gunfire, but none of the women stirred. He brandished the flashlight like a sword, moved to the entrance of the cave.

Within two feet, he stopped. Stared.

Just beyond the entrance of the cave, barely visible against the backdrop of black and gray, stood a dark figure.

Chapter Thirty-Two

Gabe stood in front of Dell, his hand outstretched. At first Dell couldn't make out what he was holding. For a minute he had an irrational thought: that Gabe was there to rescue them. That somehow, he'd been able to get his hands on a radio or satellite phone and that he was there to show it to them.

It wasn't any of those things though. In his hand he held a gun. Dell's gun. And it was pointed directly at Dell's chest.

"Gabe?" Dell's voice was quiet, calm sounding despite the inner quaking. It was his therapy voice, he realized, his reassuring tone in direct conflict with the shaking of his insides. "What are you doing?"

Gabe didn't say anything at first, just took one step forward, then another. He was surprisingly sure of himself on the uneven ground.

"Didn't know I had this, did you, Doc?" Gabe said finally, coming to a standstill ten feet from Dell. Gabe's voice sounded different, brusque, more confident than Dell had ever heard in a therapy session. There was silence and in the quiet Dell remembered looking for the gun that first night. He always carried it when he was out in the woods, always stored it in the same black nylon pouch. How had Gabe gotten it out of his pack? And why was he now pointing it at Dell?

"Gabe, whatever you're feeling right now can be talked out. We can work on this together. You're not alone."

Gabe made a noise that was half laugh, half snarl. His face, barely visible in the first pale wash of dawn, was white and thin. Shadows slid over his face when he turned his face slightly, a grimace pulling at his thin lips.

"Get out of my way, Doctor," Gabe dragged the word out as though it were made of many syllables. The gun shook slightly in his hand. "Don't you realize that it was all for nothing?"

"What do you mean?" Dell asked, tentatively taking a step toward the younger man. He had no plan. No idea what he was going to do when he got closer, but knew that standing here wasn't going to help him.

"Get back. Stay away." Gabe's voice barked into the stillness.

Dell stopped moving and waited. For several long seconds there was no sound other than the wind sighing through the tree branches overhead, the sound of fat raindrops that collected on leaves above falling. Slowly, so slowly he hoped that the other man wouldn't notice, Dell took a few steps to the side. He had to keep the gun away from the entrance to the cave.

"You have been making some excellent progress, Gabe,"

Dell said. "You said yourself that you're growing as an artist, that your work has been more authentic these past few months." How could his voice sound so normal? Inside his guts were like Jell-O.

"Just get out of my way and let me have her," Gabe said and stabbed toward the cave with the gun. Dell could see that his finger hovered over the trigger.

"Who?" Dell said, dumbly.

"Maria."

"Maria?" Dell paused, his brain whirring and clicking, trying to put information together that would help but coming up with nothing.

"Yes, Maria," the words were a snarl. Gabe's face was twisted in anger, rage. He jabbed his hand toward the cave again, took two steps in that direction. "She's a lying whore. She ruined my life when I was a kid and she acts like she doesn't even remember."

Dell said nothing, took two more steps to the side when Gabe's glance went to the mouth of the cave.

"Of course, Gabe. Of course I remember now," Dell's voice was soothing. His good psychologist voice. Inside, his brain was whirring at double speed, flying through files and trying to locate the information he needed.

Gabe made that sound again—half-laugh, half-snarl. "You're lying. You don't remember anything about what I told you."

His head had the same familiar dull pounding it had had for hours. He blinked. He did remember.

"Of course. The young woman from camp you told me

about. But her name wasn't Maria."

There had been an incident at a summer camp, Dell remembered, a turning point in Gabe's life when he was at that tender point in adolescence where the spirit can be so easily crushed. Three girls had played a trick on him, one of them pretending to have a crush on him, and then there had been a public humiliation, and exposure of some art that Gabe had created for the girl.

"She ruined my life! Her and her stupid friends. They humiliated me. She's pretending that she doesn't remember, but I know she does." Gabe stood for a moment, motionless. An owl hooted in the distance and the sound bounced off of tree branches and over rocks. Dell swallowed.

"I've been watching her, this whole trip, Doc. I ..." A twig snapped somewhere nearby and Gabe whirled, gun swinging in that direction. Dell knew there was no other time. He ran toward the thin man, ready to tackle.

Addie had woken when Dell left his spot by the fire. She'd lain for a moment assessing various parts and pieces of her body that ached, throbbed, or otherwise cried for ibuprofen. Dell must have gone out to relieve himself, she thought at first. But then she heard voices, the soft rumble of male conversation. She'd crept from the makeshift sleeping pad.

Moving as silently as possible, she moved toward the opening of the cave, keeping her back pressed to its walls. It was hard to see, harder the further she went from the fire, but the pale light of the early morning sky helped her to see outlines. She saw Dell standing to the right of the cave's opening. He had one hand out in front of him but she could only hear bits of the conversation.

"… of course." Dell's voice.

There was a long pause, then another figure, one Addie could barely make out in the gloom said something that Addie couldn't hear. Her neck ached from keeping her eyes on the two figures, but she continued to watch them, moving silently over the stones, feeling with her toes to maneuver rocks.

"… humiliated … friends." The voice, angry and bitter was snatched away by the wind. Who was it? Gabe?

"… didn't know anyone was there …" the rest of the man's sentence was cut off and Addie took the last few steps to the entrance of the cave, then slipped out her right hand touching the face of the rock. Her heart hammered loudly, drilling its rhythm into her skull.

She saw a figure—was it Dell?—hunch his body and run forward. He was about to tackle Gabe. Addie was yards away, then only feet away. Gabe, distracted by the oncoming body hurling toward him, let out a grunt as the older, shorter man crashed into his middle. The men grappled for a minute and she stood in horrified fascination as a gun was pulled and tugged between them, their hands scrabbling over the dark metal.

A shot split the air, its noise stunning in the quiet forest.

Chapter Thirty-Three

After the fall down the dry well, Dell had to stay in the hospital for a few days. He'd developed an infection in his leg from a cut that had required stitches. He remembered snatches of that time with absolute clarity: the smell of rubbing alcohol; the nurse with tight curls who had come in every fifteen minutes, it seemed, to take his temperature or stick him with a needle; the taste of metal in his mouth, a side effect of the medicine. The doors—thick and heavy— had swung closed with a gentle whoosh. The hallway floors were marked with lines of different color so that you wouldn't get lost if you wandered from your room.

He remembered something else about this time: the absolute panic of having to stay in the hospital alone. His mother had been home with Dell's brothers and little sister, his father had been traveling on business. His father was always traveling, it seemed. Dell wasn't neglected: his mother came every day to visit, and while his siblings weren't allowed in the hospital, they sent drawings and homemade cards.

But there was that feeling every afternoon when his mother, glancing at the same gold, stretch-band watch she'd worn since Dell could remember, said that it was time for her to go. The first time Dell had clung to her, crying, sobbing really. Begging her to stay, telling her that he was scared. His mother had scolded him, told him to be a brave boy and not make things harder than they had to be.

After that, Dell had been too weak, too feverish to cling and cry. But inside the terror of being left alone in the big hospital full of strangers still flooded him.

As he lay now in the darkness that had descended over him, Dell tried to keep breathing. Tried to ignore the pain radiating over the right half of his torso. To figure out what was happening, who was there beyond the blackness. He could hear voices distantly, angry voices. He could feel a weight pressing down on him, like a stone. He could see images behind his eyelids: like a dream but each one instantaneous. His mother calling to him, turning from the kitchen counter, hands dusty with flour; one of his brothers crying in the driveway, plopped down among the gravel and holding a broken toy; his ex-wife, a glass of wine in hand, a frown on her lips. He called to each of them but the words were trapped behind his teeth. All he could see were their backs moving further and further away from him. Leaving him once more, alone.

"Dr. O'Dell?"

There was someone close to him. He could feel heat near his face. He tried to move, to talk, anything to keep the person nearby. Please don't leave me.

"… hurt you."

What? He couldn't make out the words. There was a sound in his head, a steady rumble. The weight on his chest eased somewhat but then iciness fell over him like a blanket. For an instant there was pure, unadulterated silence.

There was a sudden thrashing in the bushes nearby and then quiet again. He tried to move his right arm. A lightning flash of pain radiated up his side and he coughed, gagged on the intensity.

"Dell?"

Fighting the darkness back, Dell tried to focus, to clear his mind, to open his eyes. Everything was so hard though, so much effort.

"Dell," the voice repeated. "Dr. O'Dell, can you hear me?" It was Adeline. She was close. He could feel the warmth of her body near his left side, imagined her squatting near him.

He tried to say, "I'm OK," but it came out more like *Imoooooggg*. And was he OK? No. But he was here, alive. The bullet hadn't killed him. Not yet, at least.

Finally, finally, his eyelids fluttered open. He saw the stark tree branches above in quick, fast glimpses. The sky was gunmetal gray, thick clouds pressing against the roof of treetops. Dell swallowed. His head spun. He glanced to his left, saw Adeline squatting over him just as he'd imagined. She smiled at him, but tears tracked down her dirty cheeks.

"Gabe … he shot you." Her voice was full of awe, disbelief. "I'm not sure he meant to. I think he's in shock. He's run into the woods but I don't know when he'll come back. If he'll come back." Her words were tumbling over each other and she was breathing hard. "Hold this here, over the wound," she said and pushed his limp hand to a swaddled pad of clothing pressed against his chest. "You've lost some blood. I'll go and find something to bind it with. I'll be right back," she said, and was gone.

Dell wanted to ask her more but the light in the sky above him was growing dimmer. Then it turned to black and he slipped into unconsciousness.

Chapter Thirty-Four

Addie stuffed the remains of the salvageable items from the makeshift camp into a backpack. How were she and Alaska going to get two injured people back onto the trail and then off the mountain? The trek which had been challenging two days ago, felt impossible now. She was weak, the others were weak. They all needed more food and sleep.

She'd read about sleep deprivation as a means of torture. It reminded her of when the boys were small, how robotic she'd felt. The media always portrayed motherhood as a blessed event, filled with precious moments. And it was. It was also its own form of torture—the sleepless nights, the patience required to care for a squalling, red-faced infant without ever having time to even use the bathroom alone. Already her thoughts were erratic, her thinking altered, just like the early weeks when the boys were newborns. Everything was so much of an effort.

"What are we going to do?" Alaska's voice interrupted her thoughts.

Addie paused. She was slow to respond, to react. Was it

lack of sleep or overuse of adrenaline? Once again she saw Gabe's outstretched hand, the gun. Her hands shook as she cinched up the bag and fed the nylon straps through the buckles.

"We're getting out of here," she said.

"Yes, but we need a plan," Alaska replied, speaking slowly as if she were a moron. "We need to figure out how to get Dr. O'Dell and Maria off this mountain."

"I …" Addie's voice started and then drifted away. She'd been trying to think of a way to get them all out of here. But her thoughts were skewed, her brain dull and slow and stupid. If she could just get more sleep …

"I don't know," she said finally. "But we'll think of something."

"We'll think of something?" Alaska repeated, using a high, nasally tone, mocking her. "Really? Do you have another few clients tucked away somewhere? Clark is dead. Maria is injured. Gabe is gone. And now, David, Dr. O'Dell is … incapacitated. We're all that's left. Me and you."

Alaska laughed, but it was a harsh, choked sound.

Addie moved toward her.

"Stay away from me!" Alaska's voice bounced off the cave walls. "You're the reason all of this happened. If you weren't so incompetent, so stupid, we never would have gotten lost in the first place."

Addie felt heat climbing up her neck. She turned away from the other woman, took a deep, steadying breath.

"Look," Addie said finally. "We've got to keep going. No one is going to get out of here if we don't stick together, work together. Whatever your issue is with me, we'll deal with it when we get off this mountain, okay?"

Alaska shrugged and moved to the entrance of the cave.

Fifteen minutes later their camp was packed up. Addie had retrieved what was left of the food from the pack in the tree, the extra clothing had been distributed between the two of them. She'd used two pieces to cover the form of Clark, taking back the Mylar blanket to use for Dell. Clark's body was already growing stiff when she slid them over him. She paused for a moment before covering his face. It felt wrong to leave him there, alone. But what choice did they have?

"I'm sorry," she whispered. "I'm sorry that this happened to you." Then she smoothed the hair from his forehead, like she did her boys when they were small and sleeping, and pulled the flannel shirt up over his face.

The day was dim, but the rain had stopped. Drops from the tree leaves above slid down and plopped in small, unexpected sprays. Alaska and Maria stood outside. Maria stood on her good leg and used a makeshift crutch that Alaska had made from tree branches and torn strips of cloth. Addie had used more cloth to make a pad to staunch Dell's wound. The bullet had passed right through, leaving a small, round oozing hole in his back. He was lucky, very lucky, that it hadn't hit a lung or a major artery. He was still unconscious though and moaning from time to time.

"Now we'll see if this is going to work," Alaska said, her voice by Addie's shoulder startling her. Alaska tapped the makeshift stretcher formed from the two empty backpacks—

Clark's and Maria's—and extra clothing that Clark and Dell had been carrying. Addie nodded.

"Let's go," she said.

Addie squatted and hefted Dell's pack over her shoulders. It felt filled with bricks. Her legs shook but she stooped to a squat again at the same time Alaska did. Both of them heaved upward, staggering slightly under the uneven weight of the stretcher. It held though.

"Okay, Maria?" Addie called.

"Yes," Maria replied, limping toward them. "I've never been happier to leave any place in my life."

They staggered toward the trail, or where they believed it to be, Alaska and Addie in front, Maria trailing behind. There was something in the environment here that made Addie's compass inaccurate. The red arrow would spin one way and then another, until finally in frustration, she stuffed it into her back pocket.

Progress was agonizingly slow and tedious. Every thirty or so steps they would have to stop and jiggle the stretcher, or Dell would start to slide off into the undergrowth. Maria didn't complain but Addie could hear a soft moan or quick intake of breath every few steps.

Finally, they re-emerged onto the trail. Addie would have expected whoops of delight, but they were too tired to muster more than wan smiles. They started downward, painstakingly slow. The path was easier to traverse than the thick undergrowth and tree branches of the forest. But the steeper pitch required more focus and leg strength. After forty-five minutes, Addie called for a rest.

She and Alaska gently lowered the stretcher to the ground and Maria collapsed onto a fallen tree nearby, her face a grimace of pain as she straightened her injured leg out before her. They didn't speak. The dimness was giving way to a sort of overcast glow above.

Alaska wordlessly unwrapped a protein bar, broke it into three pieces and handed the sections to Addie and Maria. They chewed, sipping water between the dry bites and listening to the sounds of the forest. The birds chirped, oblivious to the group's plight, and nearby a squirrel chattered.

Addie rested with her back against a tree. The sky above was tumultuous, the clouds moving and swirling into variations of gray. Her eyelids grew heavy and she blinked twice, tried to keep them open. Sleepiness washed over her in waves. The air was chilly but her chin tucked into her chest captured breath in a warm pocket. Nearby, Alaska and Maria talked quietly, their voices a soft murmur. Her eyelids closed. She didn't dream, but her thoughts tangled between the past and present. There were images of her boys and their camping trips as a young family mixed with present day clients and the sunny spot near the door where their old cat used to like to nap in the sun …

Minutes later she heard movement in the trees behind her. Her eyes flew open. The sound came again, louder and closer. She was up on her feet, her hand reaching for a stick or branch to use as a weapon. Maria and Alaska too, were looking toward the sound. Addie glanced at them. Their faces were pale, their lips taut. Maria looked from the woods to Addie, wildly, then back again.

A fat squirrel ran from the undergrowth, its cheeks stuffed full of nuts. A second one, not as big, followed close behind. This one was angry and began chattering loudly, apparently accusing the first of stealing food. Addie started to laugh and couldn't stop. Breath hiccupping in her chest, she finally wiped her eyes and looked up. Alaska and Maria were staring at her with wide eyes.

Chapter Thirty-Five

Dell moaned on the cot and Addie went to his side. He was pale, his cheeks and neck scratched. His eyelids fluttered once, twice, then opened and stayed open.

"Dell?" she moved closer, grasping his cold hand in her warmer one. "Can you hear me?"

He nodded, slowly as though it was a great effort.

"Are you in pain?"

Another nod, but a slight, twisted smile followed it.

"We're on our way out. Maria and Alaska are here with us, and we're back on the trail. It won't be long before we're back at the parking lot."

Her voice sounded full of false cheer but she hoped that Dell was so out of it that he wouldn't notice. He tried to smile again, but it slid off his face and then his eyes closed again. She put a hand to his forehead automatically. It was hot.

The other two women had come closer, Alaska hanging back slightly, her arms crossed over her chest.

"Is he … does he need anything?" Maria asked. She was leaning against a nearby sapling, grimacing against the pain in her own leg.

"He's feverish. But the sooner we get him out of here and into the van, the better. He needs medical attention, more than we can give him out here," said Addie.

"If we could find some yarrow, we could put it on the wound. It's good to draw out infection," Maria said.

Addie looked at her, hoping that the surprise she felt wasn't showing itself.

It must have because Maria shrugged slightly, smiled. "I wasn't always a homebody," was all that she said.

"Does it grow around here?" Addie asked.

Maria nodded, then looked around, shaking her head. "I'm not sure. I'll look for—"

Alaska broke in, "We've got to get moving. There could be more rain on the way." She nodded toward the thick clouds swirling overhead and then pointed to the east. "That doesn't look good."

A bank of blackish clouds had formed like a wall in the sky. They weren't moving that Addie could see, but Alaska was right. She nodded, glanced back at Maria.

"Ready?" she asked.

"Ready."

Alaska grunted as she squatted at her end of the stretcher. Together they hefted upward. Addie's legs moaned, but she started shuffling, forward. While the trail was easier to maneuver than the dense underbrush had been, the downhill incline was much harder to manage. Loose stones littered the trail which was washed to bare, smooth soil in some spots. Other areas were slick, with mud caked into the small craters and holes where stones had loosened and rolled during the hard rain. Tree roots, exposed and rough, crisscrossed parts of the path, daring to be tripped over.

"Addie?"

The stretcher jerked once under her hands and she gasped, nearly losing her grip. She yanked upward just in time to keep Dell from sliding off. She stopped walking, her breath coming fast, and turned, craning to look over her shoulder while keeping the stretcher somewhat level.

"I'm sorry. I have to stop, just for a moment. The brace is slipping," Maria said.

Addie nodded even though she wanted to scream with impatience. She wanted out of here, off of this mountain, out of these woods, away from the cave. She wanted to run—despite the lead pipes that had become her legs—far away from this place.

"Sure," she said. "Do you need help?"

Maria nodded, gratefully, and sank to a nearby boulder, propping her injured leg out in front of her. Addie and Alaska lowered the stretcher. She could hear the other woman muttering under her breath and caught the words, "getting back," and "ridiculous," but didn't ask her to speak up. She got the gist of what she was saying and hoped Maria hadn't overheard.

"I've got to pee," Alaska said, and headed to the left of the trail, cutting through branches and undergrowth.

"Don't go too far," Addie called, without thinking. Alaska didn't respond, just crashed forward into the undergrowth. Addie adjusted the stretcher slightly to make it more stable, then walked to Maria and began to undo the makeshift splint.

"You're doing so well, Maria. We'll be out of here before you know it." Addie spoke softly. She could feel the younger woman trembling. Her eyes were closed and her breath came in short, soft gasps as Addie adjusted the splint and began re-tightening the straps that held it in place.

"Will we?" Maria asked finally, opening her eyes. They were the color of hot cocoa and opened wide. "Will we ever get out of here?"

"Of course," Addie said. "The hard part is over. Now we just have to walk, right? One foot in front of the other and we'll do it."

Maria said nothing for a moment. Her gaze took in their surroundings: the boulders, the trees, the thick undergrowth off of the trail, the rocky, twisting path in front of them. Finally, she said, "Right."

"I didn't have a chance to tell you before, but I'm sorry, so sorry, for everything that's happened this weekend. If I had known I never would have …"

"It's not your fault," Maria said, her slim hand reaching out to Addie. She put it on Addie's forearm and Addie could feel the warmth of it through her jacket sleeve. "None of this is your fault. I just …" Maria broke off, her eyes filling with tears. "I just want to go home."

"I'll get you there, Maria, I swear it, or die trying," Addie tried to laugh but failed. "Are you running a fever?" She covered the younger woman's hand with her own. It was burning hot.

"Maybe. I'm feeling warm for the first time this weekend." Maria smiled tiredly.

Addie put a hand out and smoothed it over Maria's forehead. It was like touching a hot stove.

"Why don't you rest, and I'll find the water bot …"

Suddenly, there was the sound of crashing through the undergrowth. Branches breaking, leaves rustling. It was coming from the direction of where Alaska had gone. And then a scream.

Chapter Thirty-Six

Addie leaped to her feet, adrenaline shooting through her veins. Her thoughts were rushing, jumbling in her mind and underneath all the tangled images and ideas a small voice was saying, "No, no, no. No more."

"Stay here," she said as Maria struggled to stand up. "I'll be back."

"Please," Maria said, her eyes wild, "please don't leave me alone."

"I have to," Addie said over her shoulder as she stumbled forward into the woods. Tree branches grabbed at her hair which was coming loose from its braid. Everywhere she looked there were leaves, rocks, branches and things growing. She moved slowly, staying quiet and hidden. Which way had Alaska run? It must have been her crashing through the forest, her who screamed. But there was no sound now. Addie stopped and waited.

Another cry cut through the air, this time softer, more of a sob. It was coming from Addie's right. She saw movement there and stopped, then crouched down and crab-walked in that direction.

"… did you? You really are stupid." It was a man's voice, strained and high-pitched.

Gabe.

Breath that Addie didn't know she was holding whooshed out. She moved closer to a large tree, stood and flattened herself against it. The bark was scratchy and smelled of earth. Slowly, she leaned her head to the left, keeping her body hidden.

Gabe was still talking. "… don't want to but you're in my way."

Addie looked for Alaska's turquoise jacket. There she was, on the ground. Was she hurt? Gabe was standing over her but Addie couldn't see anything but his back. She fumbled in the pocket of her shorts. Her fingers closed around a small cylinder. The mace Ben had given her before she left.

Addie crept closer, using the larger trees for coverage. Gabe was ranting, his voice raising and then lowering while Alaska answered his questions in monotone syllables. Addie tuned out their voices, concentrating on moving as soundlessly as possible through the tangled branches and leaves. The rain had left them soggy and soundless, if she moved slowly.

Finally, she was there. Addie felt around the ground, moving her eyes from Gabe only long enough to take quick glimpses of the floor of the forest. There! A small stone. She reached over and grabbed it, then threw it to the man's right. It hit a tree in its descent and Gabe lurched that way, his arm out in front of him. He was holding the gun that he'd shot Dell with.

Addie knew she'd have just one chance. She launched herself forward, right hand extended. Everything seemed to move in slow motion then. Alaska screaming as Gabe swung his arm and body back toward her. Addie's finger pressing down on the small button of the cylinder. His head snapping back when the spray hit him fully in the eyes and mouth when it dropped open in surprise. And then the shot that broke the quiet forest with a furious blast.

Addie stood, frozen in shock and horror as she saw a bloom of red spread across the front of Alaska's jacket. She sprang forward, toward Alaska, dropping the mace and placing both hands over the wound. It was too late.

Alaska's eyes faded from light to dull until she stared up at the sky blankly. Addie's cheeks were covered in wetness. Tears? Blood? She didn't know. Her ears felt muffled as though giant hands had been clamped over them. She turned, still on her knees beside Alaska to see Gabe rising from his doubled over position. His face was a mass of snot and tears. The gun was at his feet.

Addie lunged for it.

Chapter Thirty-Seven

Ben Preston paused on the trail, adjusting the straps of his pack. It had been years since he'd been hiking and, though he hated to admit it even to himself, he was out of shape. Too much time spent in front of a computer screen and too little time at the gym. Still, he wasn't totally gasping for breath. The fact that he rode his bike regularly and walked on the bike path nightly was proof that moderate exercise was good for you.

He paused, pulling the trail book from his pocket again. He'd looked at it a hundred times in the few hours he'd been hiking. If he lost his place though, took a wrong turn somewhere it would require a lot of backtracking. Or worse. He'd heard the horror stories of hikers who had gotten lost. Some were found alive, hungry, scratched and exhausted. Others died of hypothermia or fell off cliff faces or stumbled over ravines to their deaths.

Ben checked the thin line in the book and the terrain ahead of him. He'd passed a sign not far back telling him that Bull Run trail was ahead and to the right just over six miles away. He clicked on his GPS, but it still wasn't working. He sighed, then tucked the guidebook back into his jacket pocket.

What was Mom thinking? Ben liked being active but the idea of spending days in the forest with a group of strangers—crazy strangers at that—wasn't his idea of fun. And the storm last night …

He'd watched the TV weather report, seeing the sudden change in the weather pattern that had covered these mountains in a deluge of water and gusting winds. He chewed the inside of his lip and caught himself. It was a nervous habit he was working hard to break.

"She's fine," he said aloud. "I'm sure of it." The words sounded weak and hollow though, even in his own ears.

When Dell opened his eyes, he had no idea where he was. Above him, a canopy of trees framed a dull, lead-gray sky. They moved and danced in a breeze he couldn't feel. He lay there for a few minutes, just looking at them.

And then the images started to come back. The hiking trip, the group holed up in the cave, Clark … Dell closed his eyes, wishing the images away but that only made it worse. He opened his eyes again. Where was he? Where was everyone else?

He tried to speak but the noise he made was little more than a croak. He tried again.

"… llo?"

Nothing. Silence other than a bird in a nearby tree tweeting in an annoyingly high pitch.

"He … llo?"

Still no noise. He turned his head to the right and felt an excruciating pain shoot down his shoulder and chest. It felt like fire, a jagged, hot tear. He gasped in surprise and quickly put his body back into the prone position.

Gabe. The gun.

Where was everyone? He moved one foot and then the other. Each moved, thank God. Next he wiggled his fingers, left hand first, then right. Another wave of relief swept over him like a warm blanket over his cold skin. He heard a noise then, something he hadn't noticed before. A sort of *chat-chat-chat* sound. It was his teeth, he realized. His teeth were chattering together uncontrollably. He closed his eyes again. He could make out the lightness of the sky over him, even behind his lids. And then he felt something else looming over him. A presence. A figure. Dell opened his eyes.

Addie lunged toward the gun, her hands outstretched. They were covered in blood, Alaska's blood. Her hands were slimy and slippery like she'd dropped a pail of red paint and tried to catch it on the way down. Her focus was clear, though. She could see the gun lying just a few yards away, then just a few feet. She didn't look at Gabe, didn't see anything but the ground before her and the black gun so close. So close.

Gabe's hands were on her, grabbing at her shoulders. He pushed her hard to the right, knocking her into a nearby tree. Pain radiated up her side and all the breath whooshed out of her. The edges of her vision turned gray and she willed herself not to lose consciousness. If she did, all would be lost.

Gabe grabbed the gun, a chortle of victory halfway out of his mouth when suddenly, his mouth formed a perfect "o" and he froze, body motionless. Everything moved in slow motion then.

Addie stared in fascinated horror. Like a spotlight, Gabe was centered in her vision, the gray edges blurring out the surroundings. Gabe began to rise from the ground, his feet dangling above the earth six inches, then twelve. The same noise she'd heard in the cave, the sound of a freight train deafened her. She wanted to cover her ears but couldn't move. Instead she sat, watching. Gabe's body dangled like a puppet above her.

And then she saw the beast from the woods, from the cave. It held Gabe up like a puppy by the scruff of his neck. Gabe was struggling now, kicking and yelling. Addie needed to do something, to stop it from killing him. The words were on her lips but she was frozen. In horror, she watched as the creature threw the thin man hard against a pine tree. Gabe's yell cut off abruptly. His body hit the trunk with a disturbing sound, then fell through the branches and finally crumpled to the ground, twisted at strange angles. Addie screamed—now finally, a noise made it to her lips—and tried to stand, but fell backward.

The creature backed away. Addie saw it out of the corner of her eye as she collapsed to her knees. She stretched out her hands in front of her, pulling herself toward the broken body. He wasn't breathing. His eyes stared in shock at the roiling clouds above. Addie scuttled back, away from him until she was pressed against a tree. She pulled her knees into her chest, her breath coming in gasping, halting spurts.

The creature stood across from her, a broken tree separating them. It was motionless, staring at her. She covered her eyes with her hands, then feeling their stickiness began to rub them on her clothes, hard, then harder. Rust-colored smears bloomed on her clothes. Tears ran down her face. Her breath came in hiccupping gasps. They were gone—Clark, Alaska, Gabe—and she couldn't stop the sobs that rose out of her chest, beating against her ribs like winds of an angry storm.

The creature studied her. She could feel its golden eyes watching. Then without another sound it backed into the trees, turned and disappeared.

Chapter Thirty-Eight

Addie opened her eyes. Above her, tree branches swayed in an unseen breeze. She watched them, mesmerized by their dance. The leaves fluttered and danced, and for a moment Addie wished she could be there among them. Effortlessly moving without thought or fear or pain.

She pushed herself up on one elbow. The overgrowth here was trampled down, branches and small bushes broken or crushed. A few yards away she could see the blue of Alaska's jacket. She looked away, to the other area, where she'd seen Gabe thrown against the tree.

He wasn't there.

Addie rose unsteadily to her feet. The world around her spun once, twice, then stayed in place. She looked around. Which direction had she come from? Where were the others? She had to get back to them, to keep them safe from Gabe or the monster. Or both.

Gabe? He was dead. Wasn't he? A bubble of hysteria rose up her esophagus. She shook her head.

There. That small grove of birch trees was familiar. She

remembered crouching behind them when Gabe and Alaska … she blocked out the images. Addie picked up the gun and stuffed it in the waistband of her pants. She stumbled toward the birch trees, then glanced back over her shoulder. Nothing.

Moments later, she moved from the uneven ground onto the relatively smooth path of the trail. She looked up and down, but didn't see Dell or Maria in either direction.

"Maria!" she hissed in a loud whisper. "Maria? Dell?"

No response. She started to jog, ignoring the pain radiating from her muscles. She chose the downward path, avoiding the twisted roots and loose stones that littered the damp soil. Questions crackled in her brain but she had no answers to any of them. Minutes later, she saw the pale green of Maria's jacket, then Maria herself leaning on a tree near the stretcher. Dell was on it. Addie nearly sobbed in relief.

"I'm here," she said, slowing slightly. Maria turned, a large stick in her shaking hands.

"What happened?" she asked. "I heard something loud. Was it a gunshot?"

Addie slowed further and spoke with a calmness that surprised her.

"It was Gabe, Maria. He shot Alaska. But he's dead now. We have to get out of here."

Maria started crying, big tears dripping down her cheeks silently. She put the branch on the ground and limped toward Addie, collapsing into her open arms. Addie hugged her and then helped her into a sitting position near the tree.

"Adeline?" Dell called. His voice was thready. She

squeezed Maria's shoulder and walked to him, crouching by the side of his stretcher. His eyes were open, his face pale.

"How are you, Dell?" Addie asked, taking his hand.

"I've been better." He smiled, then grimaced. "Where are the others?"

Addie was silent a moment, turned slightly and watched a last, lone cornflower dance near a patch of thistle.

"They're gone," she said softly. "But you and I are still here, and Maria. We're on our way down, off this mountain and we'll be back to the van before you know it."

Dell smiled in response, his eyes already closing again. He said something so softly that Addie nearly missed it. She leaned closer to hear.

"Things aren't looking good," he said.

"Dell," Adeline patted his shoulder. His eyes opened. "Could you drink a little water?"

He nodded and she retrieved a bottle from the open pack nearby. When she got back to him his eyes had closed again so she shook him gently and got him to take a few sips before bringing the bottle to Maria.

"What are we going to do?" Maria asked after taking a sip. She handed the bottle to Addie. "How are we going to get back now?"

The same thought had been running through Addie's mind since she'd left the clearing. How could she and an injured woman haul an incapacitated man off of a mountain? It would be a struggle even if Maria could walk normally, let alone now. A familiar pinch of fear twisted in her gut, but she ignored it. There had to be a way to do this.

She wouldn't leave either of them behind.

She tried to sort the facts out, to see all the options for their small group. The best thing would be for her to go on alone, as fast as she could to find another hiker in the parking lot and ask them to go for help, or see if she could get a signal on Dell's cell phone. But that would mean leaving Maria and Dell behind.

Or she could find somewhere for Dell to rest comfortably and try to get Maria back to the van, then come back for Dell. But then what? She couldn't carry him down on her own. Her cell was dead, but maybe there was someone on the road with a signal. She could get Maria down more easily than Dell and call for help from there. She glanced at Dell. How could she leave him here? But what other option did she have?

"What are we going to do?" Maria asked again.

Addie turned and looked at her. Her beautiful face was smudged and pale, her eyes wide, her hair tangled with bits of bark and twigs. She looked like a woodland fairy, one which had taken a hard landing.

"How's your leg? Can you walk further?" Addie asked.

Maria nodded, then looked at Dell.

"But what about him?"

"I don't know. Maybe I can find somewhere off the path, someplace out of the weather in case it starts raining again. When we get to the parking area there is sure to be someone with a phone …"

"Shhh!" Maria said. She raised a hand, looking wildly over Addie's shoulder. "I heard something."

Addie heard it too, then. A grunt and then the sound of rocks clattering on the trail below them. Someone was coming their way. Gabe? The creature? Addie drew the gun from her waistband and kept her arm low by her side, partially concealed by her pant leg. She wasn't going to let anything happen to what was left of their group.

Chapter Thirty Nine

Her fingers felt greasy on the gun's stock. Addie adjusted and readjusted her hand, taking a step forward on the uneven trail, then another. She put herself in front of Maria and Dell. Could she do this? If it was Gabe, could she kill him outright? She shook her head slightly trying to clear away the cloudiness in her brain. Her hand was shaking, the gun trembling against her thigh.

The grunts were coming closer. Addie could hear labored breathing. Her throat was dry, her mouth filled with sand. She raised her arm, gun pointed toward the path. It was steep here, the undergrowth poking its fingers out over it. She saw a head emerge, then a body following. A man, tall and breathing hard, but not Gabe. She kept the gun raised.

Finally, he emerged, pulling himself up the steepest part of the path ahead of them. He was wearing a hat which shadowed his face; he lifted his eyes from the ground to take in his surroundings.

"Ben?" The sound that came from her throat was half question, half moan. Her chest began to hitch, the breaths not making it all the way out of her mouth.

"Ben?" she said again, lowering the gun to her thigh. Tears filled her eyes as she looked at the handsome face of her son. He was sweating and breathing hard and his initial smile turned into a look of disbelief. Addie sobbed once, and walked unsteadily toward him. He opened his arms and enfolded her in them.

"Oh Ben, I thought I'd never see you again," she said between gasps. "I was so scared that I'd never …"

"Shh, I'm here," Ben said. His arms were strong and steady around her.

Once, when she'd been a teenager, on a dare, she'd swum out to a small island in the lake. There were points during the swim when she'd stopped to tread water, unsure if she'd make it. When she finally got close to the shore of the island, she'd nearly swum into a rock, large and sun-warmed and solid. She never forgot that feeling of safety and she felt it again now. Her son was here. Ben had come for her.

"How did you find me?" she asked, her voice muffled in the nylon jacket.

"I … what happened to you? Where is the rest of your group?" Addie felt his hands on her shoulders, gently pushing her away from him. Instantly the warmth he provided shriveled. She looked up into his face. There was the worry wrinkle, on his forehead. He'd had it since early adolescence, the little crease of skin above his brows that appeared whenever he was concerned about something.

She shook her head. "I'll tell you everything later," she said, "and what happened this weekend. Maria," she pulled further back, motioning toward the younger woman who was standing, stock-still and silent behind her. "Maria is hurt. And Dell, I mean Dr. O'Dell, is injured. He was shot."

"Shot?"

"We have to get them off this mountain." She was surprised how calm her voice sounded now. Inside, everything was roiling, a black cloud of fear and anger and disbelief. She shook her head, trying to clear it.

"Where is everyone else? Didn't you say there were six of you?"

"They're … gone."

"What—"

"Ben, I'll tell you everything later. Please. Help me with the stretcher, Maria is OK to walk. Aren't you?" Addie looked back. Maria was standing, shivering in the chill air. Her face was still pale, her eyes wide. She was looking at Ben like he was a ghost or a saint risen from the dead. Something that she couldn't quite believe was standing in front of her.

"Maria," Addie said. "Are you able to walk down?"

Maria turned then, toward Addie. She tried to say something but it came out jumbled, so she just nodded. "Yes," she managed.

"Then let's go," Addie said, moving back toward the stretcher. Dell was still unconscious, his face looked gray. Ben was steps behind her, his breathing had slowed.

"Mom, I—"

Suddenly, a scream tore through the woods, bouncing off of trees and sending a flock of small birds rushing toward the sky. It sounded unearthly, part howl and part woman's cry.

It wasn't close though, it was coming from back up the mountain. Away from them near the cave.

"What was that? Mom, what in the hell is going on?" Ben was looking up the trail that the group had recently descended, his eyes wide. "Someone is hurt. We should go and help …"

"No!" Addie screamed the word. "No, we can't go back. It's nothing, Ben, probably just a fisher cat. We need to get Dell and Maria down to the parking area. I can't do it on my own so you're going to help me right now, do you understand?"

Ben was silent a moment and when he spoke again, his voice was softer. He was trying to rationalize with her, she realized, just like he had as a kid. Trying to get her to see the logic of his point of view.

"We should go and check, it could be another hiker in trouble. Mom, what if that was me up there? Or Michael? You wouldn't just leave us and you wouldn't want anyone else to either, not even a stranger."

Addie pressed her fingers against her eyes.

"Please, please let's just go," the sound of Maria's voice broke the stillness. Addie turned to look at her.

"Your son is right," Maria said. "We have to help whoever it is."

Part of Addie wanted to scream in frustration, to shake her fists at both of them and force them to start walking down the mountain. But the other part of her knew that they were right.

"OK," she said.

Chapter Forty

Maria's leg was on fire. Heat pressed against the skin, running up and down the area of the break like ants. She clenched her teeth together to keep from crying out when her good foot slipped on a rock and jarred the injured leg, or when the makeshift crutch bit into the flesh of her underarm. But she wouldn't be left behind.

They'd left Dr. O'Dell off of the trail in a small alcove of immature pine trees. He would be protected there somewhat if it started to rain again. Addie had spread a second space blanket from her son's pack over him and had whispered something that Maria was sure the doctor couldn't hear into his ear before they'd left.

Maria knew that the pair could move faster without her but she hadn't encouraged them to leave her behind. She also knew that covering this same ground in the next hour, or whenever they returned, was going to kill her, but tried not to think further than the next couple of steps.

It seemed to take hours, but finally the trio emerged from the trail and followed the trampled undergrowth back towards the cave. Addie stopped at one point, whispering to Maria and Ben that they had to be as quiet as possible, and fan out a little, try to cover more ground as they approached the cave. Maria's stomach churned. She wished she'd never seen the cave.

There it was though, seconds later. Looming ahead of them like a gargoyle perched on the slope of the mountain. Maria swallowed and tasted bile in her throat. Addie was to her left somewhere, nearby but not quite close enough to see through the thick underbrush. Ben was somewhere to her right. Maria had promised Addie that she would stay back, that she wouldn't go near the cave or try to help whatever they found.

The air was colder here, and Maria could see her breath. It came in small white puffs. A drizzle was starting, too, so fine that she couldn't see it when she looked up but could on her clothes. Tiny dots that looked like pinpricks formed on the arms of her jacket. Maria swallowed, tried to pray, but the words tangled in her brain. She leaned back against the tree and watched and waited.

And then she heard it again, the inhuman scream. The hair on her arms stood on end, and she gasped, unconsciously. She saw movement to her right, and could just make out the gray of Addie's thermal shirt against the green of the pine tree she stood underneath. There was something moving near the opening of the cave. Maria watched as a figure emerged from the shadows.

She stared, her eyes pinned to the sight. It was Gabe. Only, it wasn't. It was his body, but it wasn't him, not alive anyway. He moved like a puppet on a string, a marionette version of the man. His limbs jerked and spasms ran through his core. His face was pale, so white that he nearly glowed. Bloodless. And his eyes … Maria clamped a hand over her mouth but still a moan escaped. His eyes were wide and surprised looking, as though he'd just learned something he hadn't known but had been wondering about, or friends had just jumped out to yell "happy birthday!"

His jaws began to work then. Top and bottom opening and closing like the Tin Man when he first gets oiled. Something was wrong with his clothes, too. It looked like ash or black smoke was coming off of his skin, squeezing out from the edges of his clothes: pant legs, shirtsleeves, collar— everywhere there were openings the black smoke puffed out in tendrils. A shudder ran through her body.

"We should go," Addie's son whispered loudly. She hadn't even heard him approach. Ben, was that his name? Maria looked at him, dazed. His dark eyes were horrified. She nodded but turned back, her eyes seeking out Gabe. Ben moved closer, then passed behind her, moving toward his mother.

Maria's hand felt for the cross she always wore around her neck. It wasn't there. Then she remembered. She'd found it on the ground, the chain snapped after she'd found Clark. Her hand moved to her jacket pocket where she'd put it. It was there, smooth and simple and small. Instantly, she felt comfort. She didn't believe it had magical powers, but it felt good to have it in her hand. It reminded her of all the times she had sat with it in the quiet early mornings. The comfort she'd felt, the closeness to God. She pulled it free from her jacket pocket. The broken ends of the chain swung like a pendulum.

Gabe was moving again, limbs jerking. He was moving in his strange, marionette way toward them. The black fog was rolling off him now, like smoke from a fire made with too-wet wood. His head jerked to the right, then the left, his eyes bulged. Maria felt a sob in her chest. She wanted to move closer to Addie and her son, but her legs were cement, stuck to the ground. Gabe came closer, his steps erratic. One would be very long, the next short.

Maria shut her eyes. The only thing she could think was, "help me." She opened her eyes.

"Hey! Hey you," a voice yelled nearby. "Over here!"

It was Ben's voice. Maria turned. He had stepped out of the clearing and was motioning and yelling. His pack was gone and his jacket swung open as he waved his arms.

No, don't. Maria wanted to yell, but her lips felt sewn together. Everything that was happening, it couldn't be real, could it? She watched, her gut tightening as Gabe swung toward Ben, his steps jerking forward. She could see Addie through the trees, her hand pressed over her mouth, her eyes wide with fear.

Gabe moved closer, within striking distance now. Ben held one arm up in front of him, as though to ward off an attack. Gabe's mouth stretched wide, black smoke billowed out. He looked like a grotesque jack-o-lantern, mouth cavernous, eye sockets leaking the strange black smoke.

And then Ben moved. He swung his right arm toward

Gabe. Maria could see something in his hand, a black box. It connected with Gabe's neck and she heard a loud crack, saw a blue arc of electricity. A stun gun. A boyfriend of her mother's had one and once he'd shown Maria. She'd hated the loud sound it made, the fierce crackle of energy that sizzled out.

Gabe's face contorted and his body went rigid. A scream came from him. No, not from Gabe, Maria realized, but from the creature, the shadow man-thing that had invaded Gabe's body. It was the most horrible sound she'd ever heard. It was raw and red with anger. It lasted only seconds but Maria clamped her hands over her ears. Then Ben moved his arm away and Gabe slumped to the ground. The blackness rose like a cloud, hissing and making a scratching sound, and then swirled and dissipated. It flew back toward the cave, entering like a swarm of bats.

Ben stood still, his hand still extended, staring at the cave entrance. Slowly, he looked down, toward Gabe. The man was motionless. Ben lowered his arm. Maria didn't realize she was moving, pushing her way through the undergrowth until she stood near his side. He looked at her, his face a mixture of puzzlement and fear.

"Are you all right?" she asked, reaching instinctively to touch his arm. "Thank you. Thank you for saving us. I—"

"I didn't." Ben took a big breath, then started again. "I wasn't sure if that would work. I've read a lot about energy and electricity," he waved toward the cave with his free hand, "but I didn't know if it would …" he stopped suddenly. "Are you OK?" he asked, dropping the stun gun to the ground, his hand covering hers on his arm. It was warm and big and felt good. She nodded, looking from Gabe to the cave and then back to Ben. His eyes were chocolate brown and concerned, searching her face. She felt a wave of something she couldn't identity—gratefulness, concern, hope?—and smiled at him.

He looked suddenly toward the woods from where he'd come.

"Mom?"

"I'm here," Addie's voice was thin, and she moved out of the trees unsteadily. Addie drew closer and Maria pulled her hand back. Ben glanced at her and then stepped forward, engulfing his mother in a giant hug. Maria could hear them murmuring but couldn't make out the words. Finally, Addie pulled away and walked to Maria. She hugged her, too, and it felt good to be held.

"That was so scary," Addie said in a whisper. "But he's gone now, Maria."

Maria smiled into the older woman's shoulder and gave her another squeeze, then pulled back.

"We should go," she said.

Addie nodded. Ben picked up the stun gun, tucking it back into his pack before shouldering it once again. Maria readjusted her crutch and the three started walking, slowly retracing their steps.

Chapter Forty-One

It had been several weeks since the mountain trip, and still Addie couldn't keep her thoughts from straying there again and again. She was home now, in her kitchen with a pot of spaghetti sauce simmering on the stove. The scent of tomatoes and garlic made her mouth water. She chopped cucumber for the salads, the round, smooth surface welcome in her hands.

Maria and Ben and Dell were coming for a late lunch. Everything was so, well, normal, that it was hard to believe anything on the mountain had actually happened. At the same time, everything Addie remembered was now categorized into "before" and "after."

She stirred the pot of sauce and steam rose, coating her face. She breathed in and then replaced the lid, turning the burner down low. Addie remembered dreaming of this—this normalcy—when they were in the woods, wondering if she'd ever experience it again.

A slant of sunlight fell from the thick gray clouds above, shining through the glass door. Addie went to the door and pressed her forehead against it while the sun warmed her feet. She'd never been so grateful for small things, had never felt so alive as she had these past few weeks. It was hard to believe how much of life she'd been living on autopilot before. There it was again, the "before."

Gravel crunched in the driveway and the loud bark of a dog followed. Her dog. Ben had gone with her to the shelter to choose a new friend three weeks ago. They were still getting used to each other, she and Wagner, but he was already showing signs of playfulness. His eyes were big and dark and sad-looking, but he wagged his tail more and more lately, and she'd even caught him playing with a stuffed turkey she'd bought him that squeaked. He looked only mildly embarrassed when she'd praised him.

She crossed to the front door and watched as Wagner sniffed the pickup truck and then Ben's car. Addie had worried at first, letting the dog out without a leash, but just as Ben had promised, he hadn't strayed from the yard. His foster family had noticed that he was a homebody. The steps were cold under her bare feet but she didn't mind.

"I'm so glad you're here," she said loudly, loud enough to be heard over Wagner's barking. She spoke softly to the dog and he turned after giving a final sniff and jogged to join her on the porch steps. She murmured praise and scratched his ears. He moaned low in his throat and his tail thumped once, then twice against the wood.

"Do you need help, Maria?" she called, amid the chorus of "good to see you," and "we're comings." She started down the steps, only to be waved off. Maria smiled at her, her long hair pulled back in a loose braid. She looked happy and her face shone. There was something else though, something Addie couldn't place. And then it hit her, as the younger woman drew closer: peacefulness. The pinched, anxious look that she used to have around her eyes and mouth were gone. Ben wrapped an arm around Maria's waist and whispered something in her ear. Maria laughed, tossing her head back, her white teeth shining.

"Lunch ready? I'm starving," Ben said, dropping a kiss onto Addie's head as he passed by her on the steps.

Addie laughed, then looked back toward the truck. Dell was making his way slowly toward the house. She crossed the path, the gravel of the driveway biting into her feet. Dell waved her off, but smiled tiredly as she came up alongside him.

"How are you?" she asked, putting a hand on his arm.

"I've been better, but they say it won't be long before I'm active again. I can't stand all of this sitting around and healing. It's driving me nuts."

They laughed simultaneously, then continued toward the house. "Everything is healing the way it's supposed to," Dell continued. "The pain isn't so bad now, and I know it could be worse ..." his voice drifted off and Addie knew that he was thinking about the others, the ones who didn't make it back.

She nodded, then opened the door for him to pass through. The warmth and coziness of the house took her breath away for a moment. She could hear Ben teasing Maria about something, both of them laughing in the living room, the sound of Wagner's feet as he trotted down the hallway probably to shyly retrieve a toy to show the company, and the sound of popping logs from the wood stove. Tears sprang to her eyes. She hid them by spending a few extra minutes hanging everyone's jackets in the hall closet. Then she breathed in slowly, deeply, and joined the others in the living room.

They sat around the kitchen table which had been underused since the boys moved out. Tea lights flickered in the center of it, empty plates and nearly-empty serving bowls a testament to the good meal. Old jazz music played softly from the record player in the other room, the only other sound the crackle of the fire and the soft snore that Wagner made lying in front of it. Addie looked around the table, taking in the faces.

"I thought I might never do this again," she said finally breaking the quiet. "That I might never make it back here. And when we were there, lost and scared, that's all that I wanted. Just to live my normal, everyday, beautiful life again."

There was silence for a moment.

"Me too," Maria said. "I thought about how I would give anything to just have a regular day. Cleaning my apartment, going to Mass with my mother and sister even though they drive me crazy." She smiled at this and Ben chuckled under his breath. "I never expected to get another chance, not after …"

The words hung in the air, dissipating into the dim corners of the room. Ben cleared his throat.

"I've heard bits and pieces of what took place out there," he said, "but not everything, from start to finish. What happened?"

And so, they told him. First their voices were halting, their minds resisting the exploration, but then the words came more easily. Addie knew as a counselor that there was power in the telling of experiences, but it was still hard. She didn't want to remember, not the ugly parts. And she didn't want those memories and ghosts in this cozy bubble that they'd created.

But still, they went on. Dell told about what had happened when he'd been lost, Addie about exploring the cave while looking for Clark, Maria about Gabe and his rage. It wasn't until they started talking about the shadow man that Dell shook his head in disagreement.

"That's still a little too hard to swallow," he said after Addie recounted the dark presence she'd first encountered in the depths of the cave.

"An entity?" he asked. "Like a spirit or ghost?"

His tone smarted more than the words themselves. Addie fought down the desire to lash out in return, to defend what she'd seen and experienced.

"Weren't you the one who told me about the origin of spirits, that caves are often thought of as mystical places, places where spirits live?" she asked, taking a sip of wine.

"Yes. But Addie, those are myths. Legends. They're not real," he said, leaning forward on his elbows. "They're just stories, made up to scare little kids around the campfire, handed down by worried parents and grandparents in an effort to keep their children away from possible danger."

"You wouldn't say that if you saw what we did," Maria said. When Addie looked at the younger woman she saw her eyes were fierce. Was this really Maria? The same woman who worried incessantly about anything and everything in her life?

"What we saw, Dr. O'Dell, it might defy logic. But it was real," Maria motioned a hand around the table. "And it was evil. It was dark, black-like smoke but came together to form the shape of a man." Maria's hands moved gracefully through the air, forming what she could see in her mind. "And it was cold, freezing, freezing cold like the snap that always comes in January where it hurts to take a breath outdoors. But damp feeling, too, like a thick fog."

"I don't doubt that you saw something," Dell struggled for the right word for a moment. "Something incredible," he said. "I just personally can't believe that it was something from another dimension, if you will. There are too many supposedly documented accounts of this type of thing which have been disproved through rigorous scientific studies. Ghost sightings, for example, are nothing more than a trick of the light on one's eyes, or even an aberration in the atmosphere, making substances like fog or light appear to be something, or someone, that it's not."

"What about the other creature, the Bigfoot?" Addie asked. "Do you remember seeing it? Do you remember how it carried you?"

Dell shook his head. "I don't," he said.

"How do you explain Gabe?" Ben asked, sitting forward

slightly in his chair. "How can you explain his death? The coroner said that he was killed by blunt force trauma to the head and had broken bones. Lots of broken bones."

"And the physician also said that these types of injuries were likely sustained by a fall, a fall from a high place," Dell said.

"But Mom saw it happen. It wasn't caused by a fall," Ben countered. "And what about the cave itself?"

The cave. That was perhaps the strangest of everything that had happened. The cave wasn't there when she and Ben had returned with the authorities, at least, not as it had been. In place of the large stone structure with seemingly endless tunnels and caverns, they'd found only a small cave, barely big enough for four people to enter at the same time. There were no strange symbols on the ceiling. Only the remnants of a fire and the body of Clark near it. Alaska's body had been recovered too, but had been so ravaged by wild animals that the coroner hadn't been able to determine the cause of death. No bullets had been found.

Dell shrugged. "I know that my opinion isn't what you want to hear. But again, I have to look at the facts and what I know about the power of the human mind. Fear like we experienced, it spreads and grows out of proportion. It's incredible the things that the human mind can create. What we know about it, about the power of imagination and the role the fear plays in trauma, it's only the tip of the iceberg."

Addie felt a familiar tension in her gut, but she leaned forward and put a hand over Ben's. He glanced at her and his eyes had that stubbornness around the edges. She smiled and squeezed his warm hand.

Dell cleared his throat. "When we're under a severe amount of trauma, our brains do interesting things," Dell said. "There have been incredible stories about the feats of human strength during times of stress, brought on by adrenaline. These we've probably all heard about in the media: a mother lifting a car off of her child caught underneath, a sibling terrified of heights jumping from a bridge to save his brother or sister in the water below. But there are other accounts, too, which record the images and events people see during times of extreme stress. Research shows that after a traumatic event, our brains continue to process information and sear the memory in place, if you will, for up to six hours afterward."

A log in the fireplace popped and Wagner lifted his head, then lowered it back down and arched his neck, trying to find a more comfortable position.

"That means that during that six-hour window, the brain has the opportunity to fill in gaps, to create or embellish information that wasn't actually there during the event that preceded it. It's why when witnesses to accidents or violent events recount their stories to authorities later on, their stories vary so widely. Our brains simply can't keep up with the onslaught: the emotions, the scents and sounds, the feelings of terror and fright, so they short circuit themselves."

Addie glanced from Dell's pale face to her son's. Ben was shaking his head slightly, preparing to speak, but she squeezed his hand again, then released it.

"I suppose then, we'll have to just agree to disagree," she said, her voice light. She didn't want to ruin the warm and cozy experience they were all sharing now.

"Shall we bring our wine into the other room?"

Dell was the first to leave later that evening, claiming fatigue. He did look tired with gray smudges under his eyes. The fine lines in his face appeared more deeply etched than Addie had seen them before. She gave him a quick hug by the door. As she pulled away, he put a hand under her elbow.

"I'm sorry if what I said bothered you."

She smiled. "It did, but it shouldn't. Just like I'm open to my own gut feelings and intuition, I guess I need to be open to scientific explanation."

Dell chuckled and squeezed her arm, then pulled away.

"You can be the Mulder to my Scully," he said. Then he dropped a quick, dry kiss on her cheek and left.

She stood at the door for a moment, waiting to feel some of the excitement that she'd experienced in Dell's presence before. Instead she felt steady inside, without any of the fizzle of excitement she'd felt in the past when around him.

"Do you believe him?" Maria asked when Addie returned to the kitchen. Maria stood at the kitchen sink, rinsing plates. Ben was in the living room; Addie could hear him talking to Wagner who was giving little doggie grunts in response, his tail thumping against the floor.

"No. I can't. Do you?"

"No way," Maria said. "If he saw what we did—all of what we did—then he wouldn't doubt us. He couldn't."

"I'm not sure it's doubt, exactly," Addie said. "Maybe he's just trying to cram things that can't be explained into categories that can be. When you think about all that we experienced up there in the woods, it is pretty incredible."

Maria glanced at Addie.

"Yes," she replied. "It is."

"I think Dr. O'Dell, is just working with the facts that he has and trying to make sense of what we told him. He's a skeptic and a man of science. It's difficult for him to accept things that can't be explained—at least not easily—by what he experiences himself and what he can test and quantify."

"But you're a person of science, too," Maria said, beginning to fill the sink with soapy water. "You've studied the same things that he has. So why do you believe when he doesn't?"

"Let me do that," Addie said. "Sit down and rest your leg."

Maria shook her head, but Addie nudged her toward the table and she went, limping and sat. She sighed a little as she did but smiled at Addie and closed her eyes for a few seconds.

"Does it still hurt a lot?" Addie asked.

Maria nodded. "It's getting better but yes, it does hurt, especially at this time of the day." She opened her eyes and smiled at Addie. "You didn't answer my question though."

Addie smiled back. It was hard to believe that this directness was coming from the same Maria who had seemed afraid of her own shadow for the months they'd been in therapy together. It was the trip, she was sure, it had grown and changed each of them in different ways. But maybe something else, too. Ben yelped from the other room, then laughed and Wagner barked in response then thumped his tail against the wood flooring.

Maria looked in that direction, a look on her face that Addie recognized immediately.

Addie smiled and turned, starting to put dishes into the hot water. "I'm not sure why I believe and Dr. O'Dell doesn't, other than it's easier for me. I feel able to trust my intuition more, I guess. Not my women's intuition, though that's been helpful for me in the past, but that intuition that's bigger and deeper. Just that sense of knowing. Do you know what I'm talking about?" She laughed. "I'm not doing very well at explaining it."

"No, I know what you mean. I feel the same way."

The clock ticked above the kitchen sink and the fridge hummed quietly. Addie washed the dishes and rinsed them and stacked them to dry. The water was hot and the soap smelled of citrus. When she was done, she brought a kettle of hot water to the table, offering Maria tea. They sat and sipped, both lost in thought. Addie would guess that they were both thinking about the same thing.

After their group had returned, Addie had notified the authorities right away. Each of them had been questioned individually, then met together with attorneys and officers, state officials and detectives. And it wasn't over yet. There was an ongoing investigation and it would likely be months before the case was finally closed, maybe even years. Addie sipped her tea, tried to squash the flutter of fear in her chest. She wasn't guilty of anything, yet she was still unnerved. It was a pretty hard to believe story to share.

"Will you go back?" Maria asked, her voice breaking the quiet.

Addie shook her head, then nodded. "I don't know. I don't think I could but then, I've learned with age to never say never. I am still curious about the creature, if I'd see it again if I ever went back. I felt like it wanted to communicate with me, with us, but I never really understood what it was trying to say."

"Maybe it was just saying to get away, so that we wouldn't be hurt."

Addie nodded. "Maybe."

Ben entered the kitchen, leaning on the door frame, his hands stuffed into his jeans pockets.

"Everything all right?" he asked, looking from Addie to Maria and back again. They both nodded, Maria smiling tiredly.

"Are you ready to go?" he asked her. She nodded again, looked sadly toward Addie.

"I'm sorry," she said. "I still get tired out really easily."

"Don't be," Addie said. "I'm so glad you were both able to come." She stood and collected their coats, then walked them to the door. She turned to Ben, hugged him hard. She'd never take this act for granted again. "There are leftovers for each of you in the fridge," she said lightly, blinking back the tears that came so easily since her return.

Hours later, Addie stood on the front steps, hugging her arms close to her body. The thick sweater she was wearing was warm, but not warm enough.

"Hurry up and do your business," she whispered loudly to Wagner. He was snuffling around in his favorite spot by the lilac bush. There was no need to whisper but somehow the darkness made it feel necessary. Addie blew out, her breath a white cloud in the frosty, moonlit night.

And then she heard it. Far away, the howl of a wolf. The sound rose and fell, beautiful and frightening. The hair on the back of her neck stood up and Wagner growled low in his throat. It couldn't be a wolf. There hadn't been any in Vermont for many years. A coyote maybe. But this sound wasn't at all like the coyotes she'd heard before. It was lower and louder, more aggressive somehow. Shivers ran through Addie, making her arms tremble and legs wobble.

"Hurry, Wagner," she said. He forgot about the sound long enough to take care of what needed doing and then jogged toward the steps. Still, he looked back every few paces, the growl still coming from his throat. Addie rubbed his ears as he walked past her up the steps.

The last sound she heard as she closed the door was the keening and howling far away.

ABOUT THE AUTHOR

Writing professionally since 2007, J.P. Choquette has written several suspense/mystery books and is currently at work on her next. She and her family live in Vermont where she enjoys drinking hot beverages, taking long walks and making upcycled art … just not all at the same time.

Find out more about the author by visiting her website, www.jpchoquette.net.